CRASHING DOWN

H.K. CHRISTIE

KEEKSTAR
MEDIA

Copyright © 2020 by H.K. Christie

Cover design by Suzana Stankovic

First edition: August 2020

ISBN: 978-1-953268-00-6

CHAPTER ONE

HE LICKED HIS LIPS AS HE THOUGHT ABOUT WHAT SHE would taste like. An elegant blonde with curves in all the right places. She was a beauty; her ex hadn't lied about that. He knew the two of them would have some fun together. Refocusing his gaze, he checked outside of his modest rental car.

Eight o'clock in the evening and the neighborhood was shut down for the night. She had moved into a quiet apartment complex nestled amongst the wealthy residential neighborhood with sycamore trees and manicured lawns and what he guessed were 2.4 kids for every white picket fence. It was one of those neighborhoods where bad things didn't happen.

The streets were silent, except for leaves rattling in the light breeze. Not a soul outside. No fit owners walking Fido. No teenagers out having a clandestine adventure. It was a Tuesday night, all the kiddos in the neighborhood must've been at home doing homework or glued to their screens, furiously texting their friends that they'd been with just hours ago.

He adjusted himself and wrinkled his nose at the scent of stale cigarette smoke and artificial forest. The idiots at the rental agency probably thought a pine-scented air freshener would cover up the residual smell from the previous renter's smoking habit. He should've cracked the window before he'd shut off the engine. Whatever. He'd endured worse. Much worse.

With both hands, he grabbed the newly purchased camera, fitted with a telephoto lens, from the passenger seat and pulled it onto his lap. He peered up at the second-floor window where he watched as the blonde uncharacteristically puttered around her kitchen cooking herself a hot dinner. *Good for you, darlin'.* She deserved more than her usual cold cereal or protein bar.

Sure, the fact that she was on the second floor made it a tad more challenging to watch and enter covertly. But, from his current vantage point, he could see a glass slider with a standard lock, which could easily be removed with a few common tools. The wooden, enclosed balcony made it no more difficult to reach the top floor than climbing a medium-height fence.

The front entry was right out in the open with a deadbolt. A bit riskier, but that's not how he'd get in, although he could if he wanted. All it took was a little planning and a good backstory for being there in the first place. Cable guy. Maintenance guy. Package delivery guy. It was barely a challenge.

She was easy to find for supposedly being a "smart chick." Maybe her ex had given her too much credit. Despite the measures she'd taken to start over, like changing her last name and her geographical location, it had taken him all of twenty-four hours to find her. And the apartment? Terrible choice. Too many trees and bushes with inadequate lighting where one could lurk. She, like most women, probably thought living on the second floor would keep out the … well, people like him. It wouldn't. If there was a will, there was always a way.

He raised his camera and watched her for a moment before snapping a shot of her. She bent down into the refrigerator and pulled out a jar of red pasta sauce. *Click. Click. Click.*

He continued watching through the lens as she drained a

pot of steaming linguini into a strainer in the sink before retrieving a fork and dropping a hearty helping of the pasta into a white china bowl. She set her bowl down on the counter and took hold of the small pot from the stove and poured the chunky red sauce into it. She grinned as if pleased with herself for finally making a proper meal. She lifted a glass of red wine and took a sip. It must've been a rough day, but she seemed to be in good spirits. She didn't usually drink. Or socialize or do much of anything other than go to work, run on her treadmill that sat in the middle of her living room, or watch television. He'd never seen her with any friends or lovers. She kept to herself. That was no way to blend in, was it?

A rattling noise near the rear of his car caused him to jerk the camera down. His body tensed as he turned to look out the back window. No movement. All clear. His body relaxed as he told himself that it must've been a small animal, like a squirrel or a bird. There were plenty of those creatures running around the neighborhood. He surveyed outside his car once again, calming down. He'd been careful.

She didn't seem to have a clue about how to disappear or that she was being watched. She didn't even keep the curtains shut for Pete's sake. Not that he'd be able to get a good view without the proper equipment, but with it, it was like watching a movie on TV. He snapped a few more photos before setting his camera back down onto the passenger seat. He glanced back up. *Enjoy your dinner, darlin', and I'll see you tomorrow.*

CHAPTER TWO

MARTINA

I SQUEEZED MY EYES SHUT AND WISHED MY JOB WAS obsolete. I wished that women, children, and other victims didn't need my protection. I wished I hadn't received another call that another woman needed my help. Another victim in which the police's hands were tied and couldn't help. I wished the stalking laws were different and provided more protection. Wishing. Hoping. I don't think it made a difference. There wasn't anything I could do, but to do my job. *Martina Monroe, Security Specialist and Private Investigator at your service.*

I used to love my job. It gave me purpose. It made me feel like I was doing something that helped others, and damn it, I was good at it. Now it all was overwhelming. I missed my partner.

I shook my head. I couldn't think of him right now. I had a job to do. I took a sip from the flask, screwed the cap back on, and slipped it into the top drawer of my nightstand. One day at a time.

It wasn't like I didn't already have a crazy-busy week, but I couldn't turn down this woman who, according to Mrs. Pearson, sounded frantic and in much need of our help. At Drakos Security & Investigations, we didn't turn down those in need.

I pushed off my too-empty bed and straightened the sheets and pulled up the navy-blue duvet. It wasn't regulation, but it was good enough. I stripped off my sweatpants and army T-shirt, folding them neatly and setting them on the edge of the bed, then headed for the shower. Time to start the day.

I inhaled deeply as I lathered up the lavender-mint shampoo, hoping the supposed stress-relieving properties would take over. No dice. Apparently my tension was impervious to aromatherapy. It was only seven in the morning, and my whole body was already a ball of nerves. I rinsed and shut off the water. Stepping out of the stall, I wrapped my body with a white, fluffy towel and began my morning breathing exercises. Before I could exhale, a high-pitched "Mommy!" sounded from the hall along with the pattering of feet.

Zoey didn't wait for a response. Instead, she continued to shout "Mommy! Mommy!" as she barged into my master bathroom. Zoey's long chestnut hair was perfectly combed, and she was dressed in her favorite jeans with rhinestones down the sides and a white long-sleeved cotton tee with a heart made of pink sequins adorning the front. Her baby blue eyes widened. "You remember we have to leave early today, right?"

Of course, I remembered. Zoey had reminded me no less than thirty times that she needed to bring in her experiment for the second-grade science fair and that she needed my help to carry it into the school.

My first thought had been, *There was a science fair for second graders?* I thought it was great the district was teaching STEM in the schools, but then I quickly realized it was likely just more work for the parents. Well, maybe for other parents. Zoey had led the whole thing like a master commander. The day she'd learned of the science fair, she checked out a book from the library that described 101 different science fair experiments. By the time I'd arrived home that day, she and her nanny, Claire, had the entire design along with a list of needed supplies planned out. Zoey presented her plan to me like she was going into battle and lives were at stake. At seven years old, Zoey was a natural leader—just like her father. Zoey was so much like him, sometimes it caused a physical pain in my chest. Every time I looked into Zoey's eyes, I saw Jared's. I forced a reassuring grin. "I'll be ready in fifteen minutes. Can you make yourself some cereal for breakfast?"

Zoey put a tiny fist on her hip. "Cereal? No eggs? No protein?"

Yes, she was a miniature Jared.

"Just today. I promise a balanced dinner with adequate protein. Deal?"

Zoey tipped her head, squinting her eyes, and said, "Deal."

As she scampered off, I shook my head in disbelief. Sometimes, I couldn't believe Zoey had come from me. She was such an amazing, happy kid. That little girl was my whole world when I wasn't busy trying to save everyone else's.

I'd always been the protector ever since my military days, and now as a security consultant and a private investigator, I tried to be the rock for those who needed me. I never thought there'd be a time when I might need saving, but if I were honest with myself, most days I ran on fumes.

I'd gained the label as strong and brave, both before and after Jared's death. Friends and family had all said how they'd admired my strength and that I'd handled his death admirably. I hadn't, but I hadn't been woman enough to admit it aloud. I'd always advised other women that accepting help when offered was brave and to be commended.

I was a hypocrite.

It had become a daily struggle to figure out how I could keep up with my life. Protecting others. Being a single mother. A widow. I missed Jared so much my heart ached daily.

I wiped a tear from the corner of my eye and returned to the bedroom, pulled open my dresser drawer, and took out my daily uniform, black slacks, and black blouse or sweater, depending on the weather. Sensible shoes.

I didn't open the bottom drawer. It was Jared's. I still hadn't been able to get rid of his things.

I STEPPED INTO THE KITCHEN WHERE ZOEY WAS PERCHED on the seat of her dining chair, finishing the last of her Cheerios at the dining table. I watched her in amazement, marveling at everything she did. She was independent, smart, charming, and empathetic. She always seemed to understand when I needed a little help. God, I hated that my seven-year-old knew when I needed help. I should be the one taking care of her and helping her. Days like these, I felt like a terrible parent.

I pulled my travel mug from the cabinet above the coffee maker and proceeded to feed the Keurig a pod. The sound of the dripping coffee was a lifeline. At the last drop, I clutched the cool stainless-steel exterior of the mug and inhaled the scent. Glancing over my shoulder, Zoey was intently eating her cereal. I swiveled back, stealthily reached into the cabinet, and splashed a dose of Four Roses Bourbon and shame into my coffee, then screwed on the lid.

I took a sip of the spiked coffee and nearly dropped it at the sound of water trickling out of the faucet. My little Zoey, rinsing her dish and putting it in the dishwasher. How many other seven-year-olds did that?

I faced her with the best smile I could muster. "You all set?"

She pointed her index finger up. "Almost. I need a cooler. Where might I find one?"

A genuine smile crept up one side of my face. "It's in the hall closet."

"Thank you very much," she said with a slight lisp, due to her missing incisors, before skittering down the hallway and returning with the Coleman clutched with both hands. She set it down in front of the refrigerator and pulled open the bottom drawer, the freezer. Without a word, she began loading it up with her science experiment—a set of plastic bottles filled with different liquids, some now frozen. Zoey had decided she would investigate the effects of freezing on different types of liquids. I admired her as she zipped the cooler and attempted to lift the heavy container on her shoulder. She strained and grimaced. *Tough as nails in a tutu.* Jared's apt description of our daughter. It was true she was tough, but she loved all things pink and sparkly. I have no idea where she got that from.

Zoey didn't ask for help as she labored to move away from the refrigerator with the heavy bag. In fear of her dislocating her shoulder, I asked, "You want me to help you with that?"

Zoey nodded with a bit of defeat in her eyes. I grabbed the cooler and my backpack, with the coffee travel mug clutched in my hand. "Now, are we ready?"

She picked up her pink backpack covered in pastel-colored hearts and fed her arms into the straps. "Affirmative."

———

BUCKLED UP IN THE VOLVO, I RUBBED MY TEMPLES BEFORE turning the key. From behind, I heard, "Mommy, are you okay? Do you have another headache?"

It wasn't fair that Zoey was always trying to take care of me. "No, I'm all right. Just thinking about all the things I need to do.

I received a call from the office this morning, and it's confirmed: this will be a hectic week."

"Helping more people?"

"Yep." Another victim.

"That's so cool. When I grow up, I want to help people too."

I glanced at Zoey's reflection in the rearview mirror. "That's great, honey." I wanted to help people too. I just hoped I wasn't too late.

CHAPTER THREE

MARTINA

I SHEEPISHLY GRINNED AT JULIE AS WE ORDERED LUNCH IN the busy cafe filled with professional types, likely on their lunch break. Her hunched posture, pale skin, and eyes that constantly searched the room for a threat was a telltale sign. Julie De Soto had been a victim for a long time. Five years. The perpetrator of her hell: her husband. It's not typical that we meet off-campus except with victims of domestic violence. Julie is one of the luckier ones, we think. A relative of hers came to us with concerns that something wasn't right in the marriage. Julie had shown up too many times with bruises and unexplained broken bones. Too many accidents to be believable. To her family, Julie had denied all the allegations against her husband of five years. He was a prominent attorney in the San Francisco Bay Area and had a stellar reputation.

My initial assessment, based on her family's description, was that Julie was too ashamed to admit that she, an educated, smart woman, had fallen victim to his charms. I doubt she understood the fact that domestic violence doesn't discriminate based on age, gender, race, or economic status.

When her sister, Monica, contacted us, she asked if there

was anything that we could do to provide security and to move Julie into a safe house. That was if Julie would agree. It was a big *if*. It took most victims seven attempts before successfully escaping an abusive relationship. Julie was lucky in that she had a family member with financial means who reached out to us to get her help. It was rare. We hoped to get it right on the first try and initiate protective orders after bringing Julie to safety.

I quickly formulated a plan for Julie. I went undercover pretending to be a new coworker in the office building where Julie worked and met her during her lunch break. I explained to Julie that her sister had come to us with her concerns and that we had outlined a plan for her to leave her husband if that's what she wanted to do. Like most women, she had denied the abuse, at first. Despite the denial, I tried to convince her that we had extracted several women before her and could ensure she'd be moved to a safe place, a place he wouldn't be able to find her.

Most folks think the decision to leave an abuser is a no-brainer. Just leave. Walk out the door. Oh, if only it were that simple, the world would be a different place. The psychological trauma inflicted upon the victim makes it difficult to leave, and leaving was only step one. Depending on the case, it may be that she'd need to go into hiding. Change her identity. Cut ties with family, friends, and careers.

It took two months to convince Julie to leave her husband. And it wasn't me who'd convinced her. It was the gun that her husband pressed against her temple and threatened her life with that convinced her. It was then she'd realized it was now or never. When she'd agreed to our plan, Julie finally explained that she had been afraid no one would believe her, and if they did, due to his high powered connections, he'd simply get away with the abuse and maybe even attempt to silence her. I couldn't tell her she was wrong. It was a distinct possibility.

With lunch ordered, Julie removed her blazer, and the shift

caused her blouse to slide past her shoulder, revealing deep purple bruising on her skin. She quickly straightened her blouse and focused on me. It made me sick to my stomach. I asked about work, weather, and made other small talk to calm her nerves before we dove into the nitty-gritty details. Today was an important meeting with Julie. We were only two days away from her extraction. Her husband was leaving for a business trip, and we were planning to take advantage of his absence.

Lunch delivered, the smell of tomato and basil sauce from my angel hair pasta usually made my mouth water but was now causing my belly to revolt. I twirled a bite and shoved it in my mouth. I needed to keep it together. For Julie. For Zoey. For everyone.

Julie's hands vibrated on her fork as she stabbed a piece of romaine lettuce from her Caesar salad. She raised the fork, her hand trembling, and paused. "If I haven't said it before, Martina. Thank you, thank you for what you're doing. I don't know what I would've done if you and your firm hadn't come along. If my sister hadn't contacted you. Is it normal that I'm terrified?"

Concern flooded me. Had she done something to tip off her husband? "Perfectly normal." I took another bite and swallowed. I didn't want to make her more nervous, but the fresh bruises and increased look of fear in her eyes had me worried. "Has he said anything or done anything to make you think Wednesday isn't a good day?"

Julie furiously shook her head. "I don't think so. I don't think he knows anything, but I don't know. Something is off. He's acting too nice. Too sweet. He even brought me flowers last night. He says he wants to be better. He's said all these things before, but it's like he's not trying to cover up that it's not true. It seems fake." Her lip quivered, and she covered her mouth with her hand.

I knew what was coming next. I turned away to pull tissues

from my purse and swiveled around to hand the pack to her. She took it without a peep. I gave her a moment before asking, "Does he still plan to leave for his trip Tuesday evening?"

"He said he is."

I took a mental note to verify Julie's husband's travel plans; I had a guy who could confirm whether or not he had a flight reserved. Better safe than sorry.

I reached my hand across the table and placed it on her shaky hand. "This is all going to be over soon."

She dabbed a tear from the corner of her eye with the tissue and gave a weak smile. "I can do this."

"Yes, you can."

With all the details of the extraction confirmed, I continued to ease Julie's mind by talking about little things like movies and books she'd read recently.

We exited the restaurant and stepped outside. It was bright with a faint breeze. Spring. We crossed the street to return to her office building. Under normal circumstances, I would have given Julie a hug, providing a gentle touch to assure her that there was someone who cared, but this close to the extraction, I couldn't be too careful. The change in her husband's demeanor had me on high alert. Instead, I gave her a reassuring nod before taking a seat in the lobby. I put in a call to my guy to confirm Blake De Soto's travel itinerary. Confirmed. I glanced at the Timex on my wrist. It was time to leave for the science fair.

<hr />

As I TURNED THE STEERING WHEEL TO THE RIGHT AND pulled into the parking lot at Zoey's school, I couldn't shake the feeling something wasn't right about De Soto's situation. It was normal for a victim to be scared, but Julie appeared to fear the worst. The worst being her own death. It had me thinking.

What if Julie had slipped and said something that tipped him off? Checking airline reservations and hotel reservations showed he had plans to leave, but it didn't mean he actually would. The fact that he put a gun to her head, showed that he would in all likelihood kill her. Statistically speaking, anyway. Once an abuser does something irrational, like brandishing a gun or strangling a victim, the next step is typically murder. Abusers don't move backward.

I parked in the first available spot, shut off the car and rested my head on the steering wheel, taking several deep, cleansing breaths. I had to be strong. For Zoey. It was time to put on a happy face.

Walking into the gymnasium, it stunk like a mix of teenage boys and disinfectant. I spotted the table where Zoey stood proudly next to her poster and the collection of frozen bottles. Our eyes locked, and my girl grinned from ear to ear. She ran over and grabbed my hand, tugging me to her booth. Her eyes sparkled. "Look! Isn't it super cool?"

"It's the coolest."

I watched with pride as Zoey went on to explain that there was another student who had a similar experiment, but that Zoey's was more thorough. Apparently, Zoey had a better hypothesis. I had no doubt.

After a tour, led by Zoey, of the second-grade science fair projects, which varied from trying to grow plants with different types of water to investigating the effects of age on memory, I spied the clock up high on the gymnasium wall. I needed to leave for my next appointment. Hugging Zoey, I told her, "I'm so proud of you."

As I left, she stood at her booth, enthusiastically waving with an open-mouth smile. It was an image that I wanted to have in my mind forever.

CHAPTER FOUR

MARTINA

As I forced my thousandth smile of the day, I began to wonder if it would be easier to wipe Vaseline on my teeth like beauty-pageant contestants used to do back in the day. Distracted by the squeak of my rubber soles on the tile entry into the office, I discarded my silly thought and approached Mrs. Pearson sitting at the reception desk.

"Hi, Mrs. Pearson, how are you today?"

Mrs. Pearson was old school, and manners were practically everything. The perfectly coiffed hair and magenta lipstick was a thin disguise for her real force. She'd been at the firm since day one, well before me. She ran a tight ship and wasn't to be messed with.

She tipped her head and lowered her voice. "I'm fine, dear. How are you doing? Still not sleeping much? How's Miss Zoey?"

There was no fooling Mrs. Pearson. "Zoey's great. Today's the science fair, and she did amazing."

Mrs. Pearson chuckled. "I'm sure she'll get first prize. That girl is whip-smart."

My body relaxed at the thought of Zoey. "That she is."

"Anyhoo. Your next appointment is here."

I glanced over my shoulder at the fashionable blonde sitting on one of the seats lining the wall of the reception area. I returned my focus to Mrs. Pearson. "Great. Give me five minutes to grab a cup of coffee and set up in the conference room."

"Of course, dear. I'll let her know and offer a refreshment."

"Thank you."

Continuing on into the land of gray cubicles, I headed toward the break room. Not that coffee could clear my case of the Mondays. Though it wasn't totally unusual for my day to be filled with a mix of awful things like domestic abuse and stalking victims, it was typically watered down with something less terrible, like investigating insurance fraud or planning security for visiting dignitaries and celebrities. My job wasn't particularly cheerful, but I was good at it. After obtaining my PI license eight years ago, I could no longer imagine doing anything else.

After grabbing a cup of coffee, I suddenly wished that I had a stash of whiskey somewhere. Swallowing the bitter brew, I tossed the paper cup in the trash. I dropped my bag in the conference room and pushed my shoulders back and strode back to reception, head held high. If I didn't exude confidence, then the client wouldn't have any confidence in me. Lately, it was a fake it until you make it type of situation, more days than not. I continued over to the elegant woman sitting in the first of five chairs in reception. She tapped on the keys of her laptop, staring intently at the screen. I extended my hand. "Rose Green?"

Her sky-blue eyes peeked up at me before she shut the lid on her computer. She hurriedly shoved the laptop into her bag and stood up and shook my hand. "Yes, and you must be Ms. Monroe?"

I released her hand. "Yes, I'm Martina Monroe. Is there anything I can get you before we head to the conference room?"

"No, Mrs. Pearson already brought me a bottle of water. I'm ready."

Confident. I liked that. "All right then, follow me." I glanced over my shoulder as I began walking toward the conference room. "It's beautiful weather we're having, isn't it?"

"Yes, springtime in the Bay Area is lovely. I don't miss rainy Seattle at all."

We reached the first conference room, the one where we always brought new clients. The room had just been remodeled, giving it a modern feel. Faux wood paneling covered the back wall, a flat-screen monitor protruded from the other end, and executive chairs hugged a sleek black conference table in the center. I motioned to the chair across from where I stood. "Please, have a seat."

I sat across from her and stared into her piercing eyes. She was intense and confident, yet clearly frightened. I could see her darker roots, pointing to the fact her hair was not naturally blonde. She pulled it off well. A beautiful woman. One of those that turned heads and unfortunately was probably why she was here in our office. "Is it okay if I jump right in?" I asked her.

She nodded.

"We spoke briefly on the telephone about your circumstances. You believe somebody may be watching you, and now you've found something strange in your apartment, is that correct?"

The water bottle crinkled in Rose's hand. "Yes. I don't exactly know how to describe it. It's as if I can feel eyes on me. When I sense it, the hairs on the back of my neck prickle. At first, I thought I was being paranoid because of ..." She released the water bottle and glanced down into her lap. "My past." She looked up again, with solid fear in her eyes. "But then I found a note inside my refrigerator."

That is strange. "Can you describe the note?"

"It's bizarre." She shrugged. "It just said 'buy milk.'"

"Buy milk?" I cocked my head. "Do you still have the note?"

"Yes."

She pulled a plastic Ziploc bag out of her black laptop bag and slid it across the table. Inside was a blue sticky note with BUY MILK written in all caps. It was interesting that she thought to preserve evidence. "Not to be flippant, but do you need to buy milk?"

She exhaled. "Well, I was low, really low. I drink a lot of milk because I make smoothies in the morning and sometimes have cereal for dinner. But I didn't write the note. Somebody had to have broken into my apartment and studied the contents of my refrigerator. It's creepy."

It was possible Rose was being paranoid and had simply forgotten she'd written the note. "Are you certain you didn't forget writing it?"

She shook her head. "It's not my handwriting. I don't even have blue paper in my apartment or at work. It's not mine. I didn't write it."

Fair enough. "What made you decide to put the note into a plastic bag?"

"I was thinking maybe you could send it for fingerprint analysis and help figure out who is doing this to me."

Hmm. Maybe she watched a lot of CSI? "We can do that, but before we get into the next steps, tell me what else have you've been experiencing."

"I found the note last night, but since last week, I've had the feeling of being watched. Though this was the first physical manifestation of my fears."

Interesting. "Anything else?"

She shook her head and leaned back in her chair, as if grateful to finally have help.

If I ever found a note in my fridge, I probably would've shaken it off as being forgetful. She could've had the blue paper and hadn't remembered that either, but my gut was telling me there had to be more to it.

"You mentioned Seattle earlier. Did you move here recently?"

Her posture straightened. "I moved to the Bay Area two years ago, and before that, I lived in Seattle my whole life."

"Why did you move here?"

She locked eyes with me. "This is confidential, right?"

Concerns about confidentiality? "Everything you tell me will be held in confidence, especially if you tell me it needs to remain under wraps. We have special ways to handle sensitive information."

"It needs to be."

"Understood."

"I left Seattle two years ago. I was married to a man who physically and verbally abused me for three years, and one night, things were more out-of-control than usual, and he"—she placed her slender fingers at the base of her neck—"He ..." She moved her fingers down when she seemed to realize what she was doing. "He put his hands around my throat and squeezed. I passed out. And when I woke up, he was still there, but he was in the shower, and I was no longer wearing clothes. It was then I realized he needed to be stopped, and I needed to get away from him. While he was in the shower, I dialed 9-1-1. I knew that if I didn't do something, I would die." Her voice shook as she finished speaking.

Was her husband back to seek revenge? No wonder she was taking this situation seriously. "What happened next?"

She exhaled. "While I was on the phone in the bedroom, he had finished showering and ran toward me. He must've known. He tore the phone from my fingers and read on the screen that it was 9-1-1. He hung it up and proceeded to beat me with his fists." Her body shook.

My heart thumped in my ears, my blood pressure rising. I was so sick of hearing the stories. Not that I didn't want her to tell me, but these types of situations were still happening. And it kept happening to too many women. I pushed a box of tissues toward her. "Take your time, please."

Rose plucked two tissues and wiped her tear-streaked face. "I was lucky that the police arrived when they did. The doctor said that if it was one minute later, I might not have made it. He's now in jail for attempted murder. After everything, I decided to leave Seattle and start over. We divorced through the mail, and I moved here. I changed jobs and last names. I haven't had any issues until now. I don't know who is doing this or why this is happening."

Had her husband hired someone to freak her out? It wouldn't be the first time an angry, locked-up ex hired someone on the outside to seek revenge. "And you're sure he's still in prison?"

"I'm fairly certain."

"And what is his name?"

"John Mudgett."

I confirmed the spelling and typed the creep's name into my computer. I could verify his location and determine if he might have been behind the note and potential stalking. "Have you spoken to John since he's been incarcerated?"

"No. Not once. I haven't seen him since he was arrested. He pled out, so there was no trial."

"And you can't think of anyone who may be involved with

what you're experiencing? What about a coworker who may be too interested in you?" I paused. "What do you do for a living?"

"I'm a marketing manager at a pharmaceutical company, and no. I mean, the industry tends to attract some eccentric types, but there's no one who I think would do this."

I was surprised that an attractive woman like herself wasn't getting special attention from her new male coworkers. "Nobody pays you too much attention or asks personal questions?"

She shrugged. "Not really. We have a strict policy at work and everyone is very professional. There may be a few coworkers who stare a bit longer than appropriate, but no one has been flirty per se."

It could be a coworker. "How about at the gym? Or are you a part of any organizations?"

She shook her head. "No. I don't go to the gym. I bought a treadmill when I moved here and exercise at home. I keep to myself. Work and home, that's about it. I work a lot and travel frequently."

"Neighbors?"

"I haven't met a single one."

Hmm. A coworker or revenge from her ex or someone else? Or ... no one, and her busy schedule had made her forgetful?

"Who knows of your new last name and relocation?"

"Nobody. My parents died when I was young, and I didn't have any siblings. I had a few friends in Seattle. I told them I was moving but not where. It was hard to leave them, but they understood."

"Are you in the same line of work as you were doing in Seattle?"

"Sort of. Although I'm in marketing now, I used to be in a different area of the business."

"How are you able to seek new employment without anybody knowing your last name?"

"One of my good friends called in a favor for me, to someone she knew here in the Bay Area, my now supervisor. She gave him my first name and explained I'd be sending my résumé. I'm not sure what else she's told him, but he's never asked about my past, just my work experience."

Not exactly airtight. If someone were looking and had half a brain, she'd be easy to find. "Anything else that you think would be important to know before we start talking about an action plan?"

"That's everything."

I followed up with details like address, employer, and supervisor's name—all of which I'd need to check out. I explained my initial thoughts of getting a fingerprint analysis, assessing the security of her apartment, and investigating the notion of someone following her. *If* she was being watched, I left that part out. "Is there anything else you'd like me to do, or do you have any questions?"

"I think I'll have more questions after the security assessment."

I glanced at my watch. "Great. Here's what I can do, Pleasant Ridge isn't very far from here, so I'll escort you home and assess your apartment. Your safety is number one. I'll make recommendations after I better understand your surroundings. If it looks like you need a security detail, we can discuss it, but let's take one step at a time. How does that sound to you?"

She nodded vigorously. "Yes, thank you, Miss Monroe."

"Please call me Martina. And you've come to the right place. This is not the first time we've dealt with this. Unfortunately, it happens far too often. We'll get to the bottom of what's happening, and I will personally do everything in my power to keep you safe." I meant it. She might have forgotten about writing the note and was imagining someone watching her, but my gut was saying, *I don't think so*. Women's intuition isn't a myth.

Rose's eyes brightened. "Thank you again, Martina."

"All in a day's work." I collected my things and escorted Rose to the parking lot. Until I knew she was secure, I wasn't letting her out of my sight.

CHAPTER FIVE

MARTINA

"Thank you, Claire, I shouldn't be too late." I hung up my cell phone and continued onto the highway, following close behind Rose in her silver Lexus. My body relaxed. What on God's green Earth would I do without Claire? She'd been a gift even before Jared's death. Now, I couldn't manage life without her. Claire never hesitated to pick up Zoey at the last minute or to stay late. Not to mention, Zoey adored her. With Claire, I knew Zoey would be taken care of in the event I had a last-minute work thing, like assessing the security of Rose's apartment. Claire had saved me on more than one occasion. I dread the day Claire graduates from her nursing program and will no longer be our nanny. What will I do? Cry. Fall apart. I shook the thoughts away. Right now, I needed to focus on Rose and keep her safe.

In all likelihood, there were far too many vulnerable entry points in Rose's home. First floor. Second floor. Third floor. Depending on the patio and balcony set up, a person wasn't necessarily safer in one over the other. Most people think a balcony would deter an intruder because someone scaling the walls or fence would stand out like a sore thumb, but in the middle of the night, it was dark, and there wasn't anybody look-ing. The only thing top-floor apartments do is provide a false sense of security to its inhabitants. My fingers were crossed that Rose had taken a few more precautions than just merely locking the front door.

I exited the highway, behind Rose. After passing condo-minium buildings and a park with a well-kept lawn and an oval footpath, we soon entered a lush residential neighborhood with homes nestled along the hillside. Rose hadn't exaggerated; she lived in an extremely nice neighborhood. The road began to curve, lined by pleasant oak trees and what looked like multimil-lion-dollar homes. It didn't look like a place you'd expect an apartment building.

Stopped at a stoplight, I glanced at the sidewalk on the left. A youngish woman in yoga pants pushed a stroller while walking a fluffy white dog. The red light turned green, and I followed the curves of the road, surveying the area as I drove. Not a lot of streetlights; nightfall would be an effective cover for someone not wanting to be noticed. I refocused on Rose's vehicle that now had its left turn signal activated. Blinker on, I continued left onto the two-lane road down the hill. I still didn't see any sign of an apartment building. Rose turned left again, as did I, and sure enough, a small apartment complex with, at most, fifty units was nestled amidst all the beautiful homes. Quiet. Secluded. I wonder how Rose had found the place. A real estate agent? Craigslist? I'd be sure to ask.

I watched Rose pull into her parking stall before finding a spot in the designated visitor area. I stepped out of my car and glanced around. Two different people in athletic wear were walking dogs on opposite sides of the complex. I motioned for Rose to head up to her apartment without me. I wanted to hang back to see if anyone was out and watching her.

No one else was outside other than the two dog walkers. It

was early afternoon; most folks were probably still at work. I followed Rose's trail toward her creme-colored, two-story apartment building.

The patios and balconies were enclosed and made of wood. Easy to climb and be hidden once over the top. My steps were silent as I continued down the walkway and up a cement staircase with a metal handrail. The space was too open for my liking. Anybody could walk up the stairs and gain access to all the apartments on the second floor. They would be very visible, but if they blended in, it didn't matter too much. From what I'd seen so far, all you had to do to pass for a local was to be Caucasian and dress like you were headed for the gym.

I passed the first two apartment doors and knocked lightly on the third, Rose's door. A light shuffle sounded from the other side of the door before the deadbolt was disengaged. The door crept open. Rose gave a sheepish grin, stepped back, and said, "Hey, come on in."

I entered and surveyed the entry of the apartment. From this view, I spied the living room with her treadmill and sofa and a dining room and kitchen to the left. It was small but decorated tastefully. Modern. Clean. I turned around and shut the door. I studied the standard apartment-issued deadbolt on the top and regular lock on the bottom. She'd need a chain and a motion sensor with an alarm. It wouldn't necessarily stop an intruder, but it may surprise them by the sound it would make, and it would alert Rose if the door were opened. I'd recommend a sensor for all windows and doors, which were cheap and easy to install. Easy enough. We'd take care of that tonight.

Rose was frozen in the corner near the kitchen, hunched into her shoulders. "What do you think? Am I secure?"

Nobody's ever really secure.

"I have some preliminary recommendations, but give me a

few minutes to look around." I pointed toward the glass sliding door in the living room. "I'm assuming that leads to the balcony."

She nodded.

I walked over to the slider and flipped the latch on the lock. Standard issue. Putting some wooden dowels on the bottom track would prevent it from sliding easily if it were jimmied open. It wouldn't stop anyone from banging on the glass and breaking it to get in, but it would make a hell of a lot of noise. Most burglars don't go that route for fear of alerting the neighbors, who, in this area, were likely to call the police at anything out of the ordinary.

On the balcony, I peered over the edge. The structure was stacked directly on top of the patio below, only a six-foot clearance between the two enclosures. An easy climb, even for a child. I continued past her outdoor, teak bistro set. I wondered if she actually ever came out here and relaxed? She had a beautiful view of the hillside and pines, but I doubted it. Maybe the small table and chairs came with the apartment.

On the opposite end, a second sliding glass door mirrored my reflection. It likely led to her bedroom. I shook my head. Three points of entry, not including the windows. A stalker who knew what he was doing could've easily broken in to leave the note in her refrigerator. I reached the room at the end of the balcony and opened it up. Washer. Dryer. Nice. Behind the door was space for boxes or other large items—big enough to hide a person. I didn't like that. Not one bit. I made a note to tell her to keep the laundry room locked.

I reentered the interior of the apartment. Rose probably thought that she had found peace and quiet away from all her troubles back in Seattle. Best laid plans and all. I wouldn't be surprised if it were her ex-husband seeking revenge for his incarceration. It wasn't enough that he'd almost killed her, but now he likely wanted to torment her as well.

Standing next to the kitchen, Rose stared at her cellphone. She must have sensed me watching because she looked up and slid it into her back pocket.

"Is that the bedroom back there?" I asked.

She gritted her teeth, clenching her jaw. "How's it looking?"

"Not to worry, we'll get you fixed up. So far, everything's pretty standard. Is your bedroom back there?" I thumbed over my shoulder, not taking my eyes off her worried expression.

"Oh, sorry. Yes, it is."

"No need to apologize. I'll only be a few minutes," I said before heading to the room. I wanted to finish this assessment and quickly. We still needed to purchase supplies and install them before I could leave her for the night. Right now, she was a sitting duck with a false sense of security. Not that I would tell her that.

The bedroom was a decent size with a queen bed, matching nightstands and lamps, as well as an organized walk-in closet that most women would envy. I poked myself into her bathroom and didn't see a window. Good. The only point of entry into the bedroom was the sliding glass door to the balcony, and I'd take care of that.

I exited and noted the window in the dining room on the left, plus the kitchen and its small window on the right. I could make it safer, but it wouldn't exactly be Fort Knox. We'd block major entry points, and alarms would sound at the others. I'd fix her up with a taser and recommend self-defense training. It was the best we could do unless she wanted to go into hiding, but that could do more harm than good. One, she'd have to uproot her life, and two, we may never figure out who was stalking her. We needed to find out who it was for sure so that we could stop him for good. A temporary change in location didn't easily deter stalkers who broke into homes and left notes.

Rose stood abruptly from her seat on the arm of her chocolate-colored leather sofa. "All done?"

"All done."

She hunched back into her shoulders. "How bad is it?"

"It's not terrible. I'll go over the recommendations with you, and then we can go shopping."

I was about to review my findings with her when a knock on the door caused both of us to turn toward the entry. My body tensed; my gaze averted to Rose. "Are you expecting someone?"

Her pale blue eyes widened. "No"

"Did you order anything online? Expecting any deliveries?"

Her face paled. "No."

I slid my hand to my hip and pulled my weapon from the holster. "Stay where you are. I'll answer it." I inched toward the peephole. On the other side, a man with sandy colored hair and a light complexion, stood. I cracked open the door. "Hello, may help you?"

"Howdy, I'm sorry to disturb you, ma'am. My name's Todd, and I just moved in down the hall. I was about to start unpacking but realized I was in much need of caffeine. I pulled out the Mr. Coffee only to find I'm outa filters. I was praying maybe you would have one to spare?"

He was six feet and well-muscled. The accent implied Texan. I was about to tell him he was out of luck when Rose appeared behind me. We'd have to have a chat about her following my lead. I wasn't sure if he could see her or not. Slipping my firearm back in its holster, I could take him if needed — as long as he didn't have a weapon of his own.

With Rose now peering over my shoulder, I begrudgingly pulled the door open a bit further.

Todd's hazel eyes brightened. "My lord. Two beautiful neighbors. My name is Todd." He extended his hand.

Rose remained stoic but took his hand. "I'm Rose."

Did the handshake linger longer than normal? Or was it my imagination?

"Nice to meet you, Rose. And you are?" Todd said with a smile tilting the corners of his eyes.

I didn't attempt friendliness. "I'm Martina." We shook hands. There was something familiar about him. I didn't see any tattoos, but I sensed a hard vibe from him. Not all criminals had tattoos, but it was common for ex-cons to have a little prison ink. Maybe some were hidden under his black Nike T-shirt and matching sweatpants. "Is that a Texas accent I hear?"

He gave a sly smile. "Guilty. Born and raised."

"What brings you to the Bay Area?"

"Work."

Uh-huh. I hadn't noticed any moving vans. "When did you say you moved in?"

"We arrived right at noon."

I eyed him skeptically. "So, you've just moved in."

"That's right and I'm hopin' to get unpacked tonight. I haven't much to do, but I'm runnin' on fumes and need a cup of coffee somethin' fierce. Anyways, I hate to take up too much of your time, is there a chance you could spare an extra coffee filter?"

Rose relaxed her postured. "Sure, give me a sec."

The jury was out on this Todd. Whether or not he was on the up-and-up left room for convincing. And was Rose always this friendly? It was a sure way to get a stalker or, at the very least, some unwanted attention. We'd need to discuss this. For someone trying to stay out of the spotlight, she sure was eager to lay eyes on her new "alleged" neighbor.

Todd nodded. "Sounds great."

I studied him while Rose's went off to the kitchen. I didn't attempt small talk. I'd learn more from his posturing and physical cues. He appeared relaxed and wasn't attempting to fill the silence with chatter. Maybe he really did need a coffee filter and wasn't actually hatching a nefarious plot involving Rose.

Rose returned with a small stack of white paper filters. She handed them to Todd. "I gave you a few just in case you need them before you can make it to the grocery store."

"Thank you, Rose, you're a lifesaver. It was nice meetin' y'all." He waved and continued down the hall. He stopped two doors down and entered. *So, he really did live here.* Here I was ready to shoot Rose's new neighbor. I needed to get it together. I shut the door and looked at Rose. "Have you seen him around before?"

"No, but didn't he say he moved in today?"

"That's what he says."

"You don't think he's my stalker, do you? I mean, he seems nice and not terrible looking."

How could Rose be surprised that the stranger could be her stalker? Not all stalkers were hideous-looking jerks. They could be anyone. The probability lowered that Todd was the guy, but until we found out who was messing with her, I wouldn't rule anyone out.

"Not likely, but you can't be too careful. If you get a weird vibe at all, call me, or if there's a specific incident, call the police."

"Got it."

I hope she did. "Now, let's discuss the next steps."

I explained my findings. Rose agreed to all of my recommendations and about the needed supplies, some of which were back at the office. After explaining my plans for doing the install tonight, she wrapped her arms around me. "Thank you, Martina."

I slunk back in her grip. "All in a day's work. Now, let's get moving."

It felt good to be able to protect Rose. It reminded me of why I did this job every day.

CHAPTER SIX

MARTINA? WHO ARE YOU, MARTINA? HE SHUT HIS DOOR behind him. Rose usually wasn't with anybody in her apartment and all the time he'd been watching her, she hadn't brought a friend or a boyfriend home. He may need to keep an eye on Martina. Maybe she was a new friend or a coworker. He didn't get the romantic vibe, plus he knew Rose was into hot-blooded males like himself. It probably wasn't the brightest idea to make the first contact while Martina was there, but he couldn't resist seeing Rose up close and personal. That, and he was curious about who Rose had brought home with her. Martina wasn't like Rose. Tall, shoulder-length dark hair and she dressed in all black. Martina was hard, as if she had some demons of her own. Certainly not friendly. Not like his sweet, soft Rose.

My lord, Rose was lovely. The feel of his hand in hers sent electricity through his body, nearly causing him a physical reaction in places that would've been quite embarrassing. He sensed Rose felt it too. Her eyes sparkled into his at that moment. He had a feeling she'd dig the Texas accent.

He was certain they were meant to be together. Why else would he be on this lucky streak? When he'd seen her neighbor carrying luggage out of their home, he had decided to set up a meet as they were loading up their car. It had been the perfect opportunity to casually ask them about their trip. He hit the jackpot when they explained they'd be in Florida for two weeks. Getting into their apartment was a piece of cake. Their bed was a bit firm for his liking, but it'd be all right until he could take Rose back home to Tacoma with him. He wouldn't need two weeks to make her fall for him, but it was nice to have the cushion. He'd give her a week before she was begging him to be with her. He could see it in her eyes. *Don't worry, darlin', by the end of the week we'll finally be together, just the two of us.*

CHAPTER SEVEN

MARTINA

I LIFTED MY WRIST AND CHECKED THE TIME ON MY WATCH. I should be able to get Rose's stalker's note off to the lab before the UPS guy came for his daily, mid-morning pickup. I grabbed the envelope off my desk and headed out to reception. "Mrs. Pearson, can you make sure this goes out today?"

"Of course, dear. Is it a rush?"

"Yes, please overnight it."

I still had a thousand things to do for Rose's case, but there were more pressing matters. "Oh, and when Jackson arrives, please send him straight back. We have the De Soto extraction today, and I want to review the plan one more time before we head out."

Mrs. Pearson nodded confidently. "Will do. Good luck today."

"Thanks, we can use all the luck we can gather." I was about to walk off when I realized I still hadn't heard back from the prison in Washington State, where Rose's husband, John Mudgett, was incarcerated. "Oh, and can you also let me know as soon as the Washington State Prison returns my call regarding a request to interview Rose Green's ex-husband."

"You got it. I'll text you if you aren't back from the De Soto extraction."

"Perfect. Thank you!" I said with a bit of nervous cheer before I returned to the cubicle farm. The interview with Rose's ex could provide more insight into what their relationship was like and if he was capable of hiring someone to stalk and potentially harm her. It certainly wouldn't be the first time a prison inmate outsourced their revenge. If Mudgett wanted revenge, what was he after? Did he wish to spook Rose, or did he actually want her dead? I forced myself to push out the thoughts of Rose and her creep of an ex. I needed to focus all of my attention on procuring Julie and saving her from her brutal husband once and for all.

I was hopeful Julie would defy statistics and leave on the first try. So many women weren't lucky enough to escape for a multitude of reasons: fear, lack of means, thinking the abuse is normal, nowhere to go, fear of losing their children or pets. After being a private investigator for several years and witnessing too many abusive relationships, each night I curled up next to Jared and thanked the heavens for smiling on me the day I met him. They smiled again on the day I found out I was pregnant with Zoey. I remembered the moment like it were yesterday.

I had been about to reenlist for another year with the Army when we received the shocking news that we'd be a family of three. Jared's eyes never sparkled more than at that moment, and I'd never seen him smile wider. He had wrapped his muscly arms around me and squeezed. He was happy, as was I, but I had also been terrified at the prospect of becoming a mother. We had, of course, discussed having children, Zoey just happened to be about a decade early. Jared had quickly assured me that it was simply our time and that the big man upstairs was probably having a good chuckle at our best laid plans.

I was only twenty-three years old and Jared had just turned

thirty-one. I wasn't sure how it would all work with both of us on active duty. Should I reenlist? What would I do if I didn't? I had plans to have a career in the military, as did Jared. And the idea of being home with a baby while my husband was gone for months at a time had suddenly seemed more than I could stomach, and as it turned out, Jared hated the idea of being away from the baby and me, too. We jumped into planning mode for a new and improved life plan.

Jared had explained that Stavros Drakos, a buddy and an ex-special ops team member, was always looking for talent at his security and investigations firm. Jared told me about the work Stavros was doing, some altruistic and some to pay the bills. I was interested in the idea of joining up with Stavros immediately. Jared said he was into the idea for himself as well. As much as I hated the notion of raising our child mostly alone, I was also concerned about Jared leaving the Army. He loved his job. He loved his country. He believed in the work they did. He'd insisted that leaving the military wasn't a sacrifice. "Our family is my number one priority," he had told me.

My heart sank at the memory of his declaration. The one-year anniversary of Jared's death was approaching fast. My nose tingled, and I knew what that meant. I swallowed and reached down into my backpack for the small flask I'd hidden in the inner pocket. Bent over, I took a few quick swigs and let the whiskey do its magic. The burn in my belly told me it was working.

I couldn't fall apart now. Not today. Not at work. At Drakos Securities & Investigations, I had to be a pillar of strength, and I needed to stay that way. I tucked the flask back and sat up in my chair, wiping the tiny tear that had escaped. My body went rigid when I heard a low voice behind me. "Martina."

I glanced up at Jackson and forced a weak smile. "Great, you're here. Ready for today?"

"Yes, ma'am."

"Good to hear. Can you gather the rest of the team in conference room one? I'll meet you there in a minute."

"Yes, ma'am."

Another ex-army recruit of Stavros's, Jackson had also served with Jared. They'd all been very supportive when he'd passed. Stavros said they were a family and anyone of Jared's was one of theirs. I did my best to compose myself and headed toward the conference room.

With all eyes on me, I stood at the front of the screen that displayed the extraction checklist. "Thank you all for being here. Let's do a quick overview of the plan one last time before we leave for the De Soto residence. As you can see, we are ready. One, we've received confirmation that her husband left for the airport two hours ago. Two, Julie called and said that her bags are packed. Three, Julie will turn on the front porch light at nine thirty, signaling the all clear. We're expecting a smooth extraction and shouldn't encounter any issues, but we need to be fast. We can't confirm whether or not he has cameras or if someone's watching her while he's out of town. If her husband is tipped off, we want to be gone before he can hang up the phone. It's ten after nine, and we have a twenty-minute drive. Before we go, are there any questions?"

Nods and confident stares filled the silent room.

"Excellent. Let's go."

Adrenaline coursed through my veins, and I proceeded to lead the team to the parking garage and then toward Julie's home. As my team and I drove in silence, I thought about the work we did. I liked to think it was a meaningful job. We weren't always saving a woman from a bad situation, sometimes it's our boring moneymaker cases like a cheating spouse or insurance fraud, but today was a day to be proud. Not to mention, I could check it off my to-do. I wanted Julie safe and then to refocus all my attention on Rose's safety. Something in my gut was saying Rose needed help more than she realized. The security measures at her apartment were a bandaid, and she needed a cure.

And of course, there was Zoey's campout with her Brownie troop next week. My to-do never seemed to end, but I couldn't let my girl down. She had been talking about the trip for months. She'd begged me to chaperone, citing my outdoors skills from my Army days. Sometimes I wondered if Zoey would grow up to be a super salesperson. That girl could sell ice to an Eskimo. Admittedly, a weekend away from the rest of the world with a bunch of seven-year-old girls learning how to make s'mores for the first time sounded like heaven right about now.

I made a right onto Julie's suburban street and pulled up in front of her house. Putting the Yukon in park, I eyed the front porch. My heart nearly stopped and a "No" escaped from my lips. I exited the vehicle, keys still in the ignition, and ran toward Julie's front door.

CHAPTER EIGHT

MARTINA

STEPS AWAY FROM THE DOOR OF JULIE'S TWO-STORY RANCH style home, I paused to assess the situation, blood pounding in my ears. My partner, Angela, ran up behind me, waiting for my cue. Julie might have forgotten to turn on the porch light, but the sinking feeling in my gut said otherwise. I turned to Angela and spoke quietly. "Something's not right."

She nodded gravely.

It wasn't necessary to explain that. Angela knew. They all did. I swallowed the anger and frustration. "Stay back until I give you the signal."

Angela nodded.

I moved forward and knocked on the door, causing it to creak open. I didn't want to think the worst, but this was looking bad, *awfully bad.* I glanced back over my shoulder toward Angela. My stare met her dark eyes. I didn't have to say anything. I waved my hand, signaling to the rest of the team to exit their vehicles. "I'm going in. Dial 9-1-1 and then have the team do a sweep in and around the house."

I watched Angela pull her cell phone from the thigh pocket of her black cargo pants.

As I pushed the door open all the way, I could hear, "9-1-1, what's your emergency?" from Angela's cell. I pulled my firearm from my hip holster and flicked off the safety. There were no lights on. The only visibility was from the sunlight filtering through the windows in the back of the house.

Gun drawn, I proceeded to enter.

The sitting room on the left looked undisturbed, tidy, full of shadows, but devoid of life. I continued to the kitchen. It was U-shaped with an island in the center, tastefully done with granite countertops and shaker-style cabinets. It was empty and immaculate. To the right, a living room with a big-screen TV. It was clean, too clean, as if it were a model home. Not a place you would call "lived in."

I turned back around and headed for the stairs. The only sounds were the footsteps of my team close behind me. I slowly ascended the steps, creaking noises echoing loudly. If anybody were at the top listening for intruders, I'd now be the sitting duck. I reached the top of the stairs, with no movement detected from the top floor.

The first door on the left was open, a laundry room with a washing machine and dryer inside. I continued down the hall to the door on the right. I glanced at the carpet and spotted flecks of reddish-brown material. Not tidy. Not right. I inched closer and stopped, allowing my team to catch up—and preparing myself for what we may find. I turned and shook my head grimly at Jackson.

He gave a knowing nod.

I stepped closer and entered the bedroom. Heart pounding, I rushed to the blood-soaked body lying on the floor. In vain, I checked for a pulse. I shut my eyes and stepped away from Julie's lifeless body to avoid contaminating the scene. I was about to tell Jackson to tell Angela to update the 9-1-1 caller when the vomit began to rise. I dashed out of the room, down the stairs, out the front door, and onto the lawn where I spewed the contents of my breakfast. I remained there, head in my left hand, with tears flowing freely.

I don't know how he knew. How did he know? Did Julie know that her husband was on to her? Had he done it himself or hired a killer? We'd had confirmation from Julie that he'd left. Had he returned? I had just spoken with Julie half an hour ago. What did I miss? How could I have let this happen? I didn't understand, and now I'd lost all composure. I was a disgrace—a failure, unable to save her. I wasn't sure I could do this job anymore.

I sat frozen on the lawn, gun still in my right hand. The fear of letting more women down in the future suffocated me.

"Ma'am?"

I didn't look up at Angela. "She's dead. Tell them she's dead." I sucked up my grief and wiped my mouth with the back of my hand and pushed off the ground. Placing my gun in my holster, I wiped my eyes with the hem of my shirt. I stood up and turned to face Angela, who was relaying the information to the operator.

"He couldn't have gotten far, I spoke with her thirty minutes ago," I told her.

AFTER THE POLICE ARRIVED AND WE'D GIVEN OUR statements, it was one o'clock. Lunchtime. Back at the office, I told the team I had to run an errand. Today, my most important errand was a trip to my favorite liquor store two towns away.

Medicine in hand, I sat slumped over in the front seat of my car and thought about all the people I hadn't saved. I hadn't saved Julie. I hadn't saved Jared. *Oh, Jared. I wish you were here.*

Almost a year ago, Jared had been working a high-profile

celebrity security detail in San Francisco. The celebrity, a young starlet, had insisted on having the most highly trained and physically fit for her security. She'd been getting death threats and was hyper-vigilant about her security and physical well-being. Still, she had a new movie opening in San Francisco and wanted to attend the premiere, greeting fans beforehand. Stavros had assigned the best members of the team, which of course had included Jared.

I'd been at a Brownie meeting with Zoey and her troop. She had been so excited to be old enough to join the Girl Scouts. As she put it, she wanted to sell cookies and learn skills. Impressed by her enthusiasm, I had taken the afternoon off to attend the meeting with her. We were speaking to the troop leader when my cell phone buzzed, and I saw that it was Stavros calling, so I'd politely excused myself. Out in the hall of the elementary school, with a sense of dread in my core, I answered.

I remember the conversation like it was yesterday.

"Stavros, what's up?"

"Where are you, Martina?"

My body froze. It was never a question you wanted to be asked by your boss, who was not only ex-special forces but an expert in crisis management. He and I knew never to give someone bad news if they're driving or engaged in an activity that if their attention was taken away, could cause them harm. I swallowed. "I'm at Zoey's school for her Girl Scout troop meeting. What's going on?"

"There's been an accident."

My stomach flipped. I leaned up against the wall to steady myself. "How bad is it?"

Silence. Too much silence. "Who was it?" It was always a bad day when we lost one of the team. We didn't lose many, but when we did, it hit us hard.

"It was Jared."

I'd shook my head. "No, it couldn't be."

"I'm so sorry. There was nothing they could do. They hit the carotid."

My knees weakened, and I'd used the building as a crutch as I melted down into a ball on the cold cement. Not Jared. Anybody but Jared. "Are you sure?"

"I was there."

I couldn't speak. I couldn't breathe. Tears flooded. My vision blurred. Everything was fuzzy. The trees, the walls, everything wouldn't stop moving. I propped myself onto my knees, trying to get air. Trying to steady myself. I kept hearing in my ear, "Martina? Martina? Are you okay?"

I fell back against the wall. "I'm here."

"You want me to have someone come and pick up you and Zoey?"

Suddenly, my training kicked in. I wiped my face and stood. "That won't be necessary."

I needed to see Jared. His body. His face. I couldn't bring Zoey. "I'm going to call the sitter and have her take care of Zoey. Where is he?"

"He's at San Francisco General."

"All right, I'll get things settled with Zoey, and then I'll be over. Be there in an hour."

"I'd feel better if we sent a car."

"I'll be fine," I spat. "I'll see you in an hour."

Stavros had created a foursquare formation around the celebrity, but they kept their distance to make sure she could still be photographed easily by fans. Jared had caught sight of the shooter and lunged in front of the star to protect her.

Always the protector.

I always loved that about him, but that day I didn't love it. I didn't want him to protect some stranger, some celebrity. I wanted him to continue to protect our family — our daughter. The shooter let off one shot before the other men on the security detail took him down. The doctor had said it was an unlucky hit to the neck, damaging the carotid. Jared bled out in minutes.

In those minutes, my world was altered forever.

I didn't know how to live without Jared. I didn't know how to be a single parent. I didn't know how to explain to our six-year-old daughter that her hero, her daddy, was gone and never coming back. At that moment, I didn't know how I would do anything, but I knew that I had to, for Zoey.

And now, once again, I didn't know how I'd continue. It was all so much harder than I thought it would be. It turns out I wasn't as strong as I thought, and it made me sick.

CHAPTER NINE

MARTINA

MY HEAD POUNDED AND MY STOMACH SOURED. AFTER Zoey went to sleep last night, I had finished off the bottle of whiskey, needing to calm my nerves and allow myself to drift away from all the stress and ugliness. I grabbed my head, letting it fall forward in my hands. Consuming the rest of the whiskey hadn't been the best decision. Cold sweat covered my neck and chest.

It was another rough morning. What I would've given to sleep through the night or be able to get some shut-eye without alcohol. I hadn't in almost a year.

In a weak moment I'd considered going to a therapist and getting myself a prescription for sleeping pills, but I didn't want people to know I was struggling. I was a soldier. I'd seen combat. Surely I could handle grief, loneliness, and being a single parent. I was trained to be strong. I had to remain that way.

My shoulders drooped. I had told myself this feeling was temporary, and eventually, it would get better. I could handle temporary. Approaching the one-year anniversary of losing my love and my partner, I began to question whether or not that temporary fix was still doing the trick. Losing Julie had pushed me an inch closer to the line.

My head swirled with emotions.

Anger.

Sadness.

Guilt.

Fear.

Fear that I would fail again and another person would die. Fear that I would lose Zoey. Fear that I had already lost myself.

I pressed the button on the Keurig and glanced over at Zoey sitting at the kitchen table. Her headband made of pink sequins shimmered as she bobbed her head around, speaking a mile a minute about the class pet that she couldn't wait to bring home: a snake. That was all I needed — a literal snake in my house. Whose bright idea was it to have the class pet be a snake? Yuck. Was Zoey more excited about bringing the snake home or her chance to feed it live mice? Double yuck.

I wondered at what point she'd take a breath from her long speech describing the snake and its shimmering scales, alas, she continued. "It's okay that the snake eats mice. The rodents aren't the cute kind. Plus, it's the circle of life. It's completely natural," she explained.

I nodded. "That's true." Boy, Zoey definitely had the gift of gab, and thank goodness she did. If it weren't for Zoey, our house would be all but dark and silent. Maybe that's why God had made Zoey sparkly, not only on the outside but on the inside too. Before Zoey, Jared and I liked to have a good time, but we were both known for our seriousness and determination. But once Zoey came along, I delighted in watching Jared tease and tickle her until they were both stuck in a fit of giggles. It had been a side of him I hadn't seen before her arrival. I held my breath as it felt like a knife cut through my chest. How had I ever thought I could do this life without him?

Sometimes I wondered if Zoey would be better off without me.

I grabbed the full cup of coffee and took a sip. *You just have to get through this week,* I told myself. The anniversary. A year without my husband. A year of being a single parent. A year where each day I feared I might drown.

"So, what do you think?"

I had no idea what Zoey had asked. "What?"

She let out a dramatic sigh. "Mommy, you're not being a good listener."

No, I wasn't. Lately, I wasn't being good at *anything.* "You're right. I'm sorry. What were you asking me?"

"The snake, can we bring her home next week?"

The snake. Her innocent pleading eyes made it seem like bringing home a snake would be better than Christmas. How could I say no to that? "Sure, that's fine."

Her face brightened with a huge grin. "Cool. Oh, and you know what is super cool?"

Was I ready to hear this? "No, what?"

"Kayla is bringing Mitzy, that's the snake, home on Friday, so when I'm at her house for the sleepover, I'll get to play with her. When she comes home with us, she'll already know me!"

"That is cool."

Yes, the sleepover at Kayla's. Zoey loved a good sleepover, especially with her best friend, Kayla. Before I could dive into more dark thoughts, Zoey practically squealed. "I'm so excited!"

Yes, Zoey had a sleepover while I had to attend Jared's celebration of life. I had opted to have her stay over at her best friend's house instead of taking her to a restaurant where Jared's brother and parents and people from the office, including Stavros, would be gathering to celebrate his life. The one-year anniversary of his death. I hadn't reminded Zoey that her daddy had been gone for a year. Neither one of us needed to be reminded. His absence reminded us every single day.

I hadn't planned anything for the day, but Stavros and Jared's ex-soldier pals said that's how they honor their own. "We never forget," they had said. How could I ever forget when I lived with a gaping hole in my life? On Friday, it wouldn't be easy to fake a smile, but then again, it never was.

"Cool! Ha!" Zoey exclaimed. I had no idea what she was going on about, but apparently, my blank expression had been a dead giveaway that my attention was elsewhere. "Mommy, this is the second time this morning you aren't being a good listener."

Only twice? Maybe I was better off than I thought. "I'm so sorry, sweetie. What were you saying?"

"I *said* over at Kayla's we're going to watch a movie and eat popcorn and pizza. Doesn't that sound fantastic?"

Despite feeling half-dead inside, a grin crept up my face. To be thrilled about something as normal as movies, pizza, and popcorn at your best friend's house wasn't something you could buy. Placing my coffee down, I tiptoed over to Zoey, with a mischievous look. "It does sound fantastic. I'm so jealous!" I snuck my hands under her armpits for a tickle attack, and Zoey giggled uncontrollably. It was the best sound in the whole world. I stood back after I felt the vibration of my cell phone in my pocket. I removed it and studied the screen. Dread filled my insides.

I kissed her on her soft cheek and said, "Finish your breakfast, honey. I have to take this call, and I'll need quiet. Okay?"

Zoey pinched her fingers together and zipped her mouth closed. I gave her a thumbs up and headed toward the hallway. "This is Martina Monroe."

"Martina, it's Rose."

Her voice was shaky.

My stomach balled up tight. "What's going on, Rose?"

My nerves rattled as she explained that somebody had broken into her apartment at two in the morning. They'd gotten past the chain lock, but the alarm had alerted her to the intruder. By the time she'd rushed out of bed, the perpetrator was gone.

"Did you notify the police?"

"Yes, I called them right after it happened. They told me I was lucky because the alarm probably spooked whoever was trying to break in, but I'm not feeling very lucky."

"What did they do to investigate?" *Damn.* I could've lost Rose too. I needed to get it together; I couldn't handle another person's death on my hands.

"They dusted for prints and said they would ask the neighbors if they'd seen anything. One officer suggested putting another lock on the door; he thinks maybe the intruder had a key. They said that if I was feeling unsafe, I should stay at a hotel."

The escalation of her stalker wasn't a good sign. He or she had to have known Rose was home. As I was passed out from the booze last night, Rose could've been killed or raped or assaulted. I clenched my teeth together. Rose's case needed to top priority. I'd suggest a team be assigned to her twenty-four hours a day until we caught this guy. I didn't care what it cost, and Stavros wouldn't either.

From this moment forward, I'd devote all my time to keeping Rose safe. I couldn't lose another client.

"Can you meet me at my office so we can discuss this further? I have to drop my daughter off at school, but I can be there by nine."

"Yes, I'll be there."

This should've never happened. Rose shouldn't be in

danger. After coming to me, she should've been safe. It was my job. I needed to fix this, and fast. I'd been too preoccupied with everything else, I was slipping. I needed to get my head on straight before somebody else got hurt.

CHAPTER TEN

HE TUGGED DOWN ON THE BRIGHT BLUE WARRIORS BALL
cap and slipped on his sunglasses, concealing the majority of his
face. At this point, he couldn't be too careful. After the flub
earlier that morning, he needed to ensure that nothing would
stand in the way of Rose and him being together. Up until that
point, he'd been sure he'd been invisible to Rose, but knowing
she'd installed an alarm and chain lock at her front door, he realized he hadn't been.

As he peered up from his vehicle, he couldn't see through
her shut curtains. She must have received his message and
hadn't taken it as intended. It was supposed to make her feel like
someone was looking out for her, not someone out to harm her.
This morning's debacle of police involvement would make his
goal of being with Rose trickier, but not impossible. He shifted
in his seat and reminded himself, only things worth fighting for
were worth anything at all.

He'd sat in his car for over an hour waiting for her to leave
for work, but she hadn't left her apartment at her regular time.
Had she decided to take the day off? What if she didn't leave
her apartment? He hated the idea of not seeing her. He

unzipped his backpack on the front passenger seat and pulled out a pair of black lace panties. He bent over and raised the goodies to his nostrils and inhaled. Oh, how he loved her scent.

It had been two days since he'd been able to touch her delicate skin. He'd felt only her hand, but was sure the rest of her was just as sweet. Come to think of it, he hadn't seen Rose since that woman Martina had visited. Who was Martina? He supposed it might be time to find out more about her, but he didn't know her last name and hadn't seen her since their meeting.

He shifted his thoughts back to the treasure in his hand, and with the other, he unbuttoned his jeans. He caught movement from her front door and halted. She was leaving the apartment. He shoved the panties back into his backpack and refastened his pants. He watched as she hurried down the steps toward the parking lot. She was dressed casually in black sweatpants, a purple sweatshirt, and a pair of New Balance tennis shoes. Her golden hair was pulled back into a low ponytail. Her outfit wasn't her typical work attire. No, she couldn't be going to work. *Where are you going, Rose?* He turned on the car and eased into a position to follow her out of the entrance of the complex.

Twenty minutes later, she exited the highway, and soon after, she pulled into the parking lot of a group of large office buildings. He watched as she stepped out of her car and casually entered the building—as if she'd been there before. He waited for her to be out of sight before he parked across the lot to investigate further.

With the coast clear, he scurried toward the entrance and performed a quick cursory glance at the different buildings. Once inside, he beelined for the directory and studied the board. Law office. Doctors offices. *Not feeling well, Rose?* Continuing down the list, his body went rigid, and he stepped back. Drakos Security & Investigations. A wriggling in his gut

warned him. Had Rose hired a PI to find out who'd left a note?
Was Martina a PI? It'd fit. Dressed all in black and untrusting as
all get out. Had the PI recommended the new alarms and lock?
The wooden dowels in the sliding glass doors?

He needed to act quicker than planned. He thought, *No
worries, Rose, we'll be together soon.*

CHAPTER ELEVEN

MARTINA

I KICKED BACK ONE LAST SWIG OF MY HOME BREW AND shoved the mug back into the cupholder. I shook my head. *Enough with the self-pity party, Martina.* I reminded myself that I'd had a lot on my plate, and that's why I'd not done everything I should've for Rose. That ended now. I was a warrior. Unstoppable. *You got this, Martina.* I popped a mint and hurried out of my car toward the entrance of the building.

Inside, pumped and ready, I opted to take the stairs instead of the elevator. God knows I needed the exercise; it'd been weeks since I hit the gym, and I could feel it. I hurried up the stairs. By the second flight, I panted for more air but didn't give up. I couldn't, not now. A tight grip on the safety railing, I hiked the remaining four flights. I caught my breath before opening the door to the hallway. Nobody from the office needed to see me like this. I was now regretting running up the stairs, seeing as now my armpits were sticky, and sweat trickled down my spine.

Taking a few minutes to breathe steadier, I pushed open the door to the hall and entered Drakos Security & Investigations.

Mrs. Pearson was in the middle of a conversation with

someone on the phone. Perfect, no need to stop for polite chitchat. I waved as I passed, but she lifted her finger to stop me.

"Please hold," Mrs. Pearson said and rested the receiver against her chest. "Perfect timing. I'm on the phone with King County Correctional. You've been approved for an interview with John Mudgett. Do you prefer later today or tomorrow?"

"Tomorrow would be best."

"I'll make arrangements."

"Perfect. Thank you."

At least something was going right. Hopefully, talking to Rose's ex would give me insight into who was after her. "Oh, and when Rose Green arrives, please send her straight back."

"You got it. Take care."

I marched to my cubicle with purpose. I needed to keep my head clear and finalize a plan for Rose. Number one issue to tackle—safety. We'd put new locks on the door, so if the intruder had a key, he wouldn't anymore. One night away to get some sleep would be okay, but these types of predators don't stay away for long, and I was sure Rose didn't want to live the rest of her life in hiding. No, I wouldn't allow it, and I'd teach her to defend herself. Self-defense. Weapons training. Even if the jerk were able to gain entry into her apartment again, I would teach her to fight him off, at least long enough for the police to arrive. I'd teach her how to spot a tail and provide tips for being alert at all times. Not only could it save her life, but the ability to defend oneself empowers and builds confidence. I owed her that much, considering my sloppiness could have gotten her killed. I shook the thoughts from my brain. I had to remain positive, not dwell on what had gone on before. I could only work from this moment forward.

The sound of sneakers on the carpet caught my attention. I glanced over at the arrival. Dark circles shadowed Rose's eyes. Her skin was pale and devoid of makeup. Her hair hung in a loose ponytail, and sweatpants sagged on her body beneath an oversized sweatshirt. Sneakers. She'd probably thought running shoes was a good, cautious choice. She was right.

I lifted out of my chair. "Rose. How are you?"

"Still alive, I suppose."

"Can I get you anything? Water, tea, coffee?"

Rose dismally shrugged. "Maybe some water."

I unplugged my laptop and tucked it under my arm. "No problem, follow me." A pit in my stomach formed. Rose's usual confidence was absent and replaced with fear. It wasn't going to help the situation. I needed to fix this, fast.

In the kitchen, I filled the paper cup with water and handed it to her before preparing one for myself.

She nodded. "Thanks."

"Let's go to the conference room where we can talk."

Sitting across from one another, I said, "Just so you know, if something like this happens again, you can call me right away. You don't have to wait until it's later in the day. Midnight. Two in the morning. It doesn't matter. Obviously, first, call the police, but then call me. I'll rush over so you don't have to be alone." What would I do when Claire graduated from her nursing program? Who would help me take care of Zoey when I needed to rush out in the middle of the night?

"Do you know if the police got any hits on the fingerprints?" I asked.

"Not yet. They said it could take a few days to get the results. Maybe weeks."

False. If the police made it a priority, they'd be able to get results within forty-eight hours. The lackadaisical attitude by her local law enforcement was a bit surprising. I would've thought in a quiet town like Pleasant Ridge they would take the case more seriously, considering not a lot of crime happened there.

"And you said they didn't see any signs of forced entry?"

She exhaled heavily, clearly frustrated. "They said the intruder must have had a key."

How did this guy have a key? Did he work for the apartment complex? "Do you have a spare key to your apartment somewhere that he could've gotten access to?"

She titled her head as if to think about it. "I do, actually. It's in a kitchen drawer. I haven't checked to see if it's still there. Should I?"

I didn't want her near her apartment again until the locks were changed. "Let's hold off for now. Did the police say there was anything else unusual about the break-in?"

"No. They said that the intruder, if there was one, must've opened the door slowly since he didn't break the chain lock when he pushed it open, but the alarm sounded."

"If?"

"One cop said maybe it was unlocked, and I didn't remember, and the breeze blew it open."

"Was the deadbolt engaged?"

"Of course, and the chain in place. I checked all windows and doors before I went to bed. I'm positive it was locked."

I believed her. Stalking victims didn't typically forget to lock the front door. "Do you have the cards of the police officers you spoke with?"

"Yeah." Rose picked up her purse from the floor, fished around, pulled out a few cards, and slid them across the table.

I scanned the names, but they weren't anyone I was familiar with. I tapped the notes into my laptop with the names of the officers, along with their badge numbers and contact information. It was likely these officers would be of little to no use, but it was good to know who I'd be working with if another incident occurred.

"Anything else I should know?"

She shook her head.

"What I'd like to do next is talk about how we move forward. My first priority is your safety. You're staying at a hotel tonight while we get new locks, okay?"

Rose nodded.

"My guess is you don't have the desire to live in hiding forever?"

"No."

"Have you taken any self-defense training? Do you carry potential weapons? Pepper spray? A Taser? Or anything you could use to defend yourself?"

"Not really. I've completed a self-defense class, but it was a while ago. I usually keep pepper spray in my purse, but that's it."

As expected. "First, I'd like for you to take another self-defense class, a serious class. I'll give you the name and location of a few local studios. Second, I'll provide you with a taser. I like a good taser over pepper spray. With pepper spray, you need to be close to your attacker to use it; the closer you are, the more likely they can overtake you. Third, and now you may object, but I'd recommend firearms training. I also have the names of a few good instructors and a firing range close to your home." I checked her response. Rose's eyes brightened. *Good.* "I came up with this plan not to scare you, but to empower you. These predators, like this stalker and your ex, try to take your control, your power. I'd like to help you get it back. How does that sound?"

Rose nodded emphatically. "Really good. I want to be able to defend myself. I want my power back."

I knew I liked Rose. She had a fighting spirit; these men just happened to take it away momentarily. We'd change that. "Great, Mrs. Pearson completely cleared my schedule today so that I can work with you. Although I have some information for continued training, I'm also a trainer. Today, if you're up for it, I'd like to teach you some basic self-defense and how to use the taser most effectively, as well as how to spot a tail and to be alert at all times. There is a gym downstairs where I've rented one of the studios for the private lesson. Is this something you'd like to do?"

She gave me a weak smile. "Yes."

Good. "Great. Before we head to the gym, let's discuss the plans for the investigation. Tomorrow, I'll fly up to Seattle to interview your ex-husband and discover if he has any involvement in this and maybe shine a light on who could be doing this." Part of me hoped it was the ex-husband behind everything. I hated to think Rose was unlucky enough to be subjected to two abusers in her life. Though, once someone has been a victim of abuse, they are more likely to be a victim again. It was a sad fact, but it was true.

"As I prepare to interview John, I'd like your help in learning more about him. Family life, career, where he grew up, that kind of thing. A list of friends or family or associates that may still be in contact with him. Basically, anything that will help me understand him more. Can you do that?"

The mention of her ex made her body go rigid. She was clearly still terrified of him even though he was behind bars. "Yes."

"Excellent. Before we get started on that and discuss the rest of our plan, let me go ahead and order in lunch. We'll need it to keep our energy up." I suspected Rose hadn't eaten much of anything; she was still a little shaky and listless. I didn't need her passing out on the gym floor. I needed her focused and ready to learn. My world was already a house of cards, and it couldn't take another mighty wind. Fingers crossed, the interview with her ex-husband would provide some insight into who was terrorizing her, so I could stop them, and fast.

CHAPTER TWELVE

MARTINA

I STARED INTO HIS DEEP BLUE EYES AS HE TOLD ME A woeful story of his wrongful conviction. With a muscular physique and sculpted dark hair, it was clear John Mudgett had been taking care of himself while in prison. He appeared charming with a kind smile. Not a person one would typically expect to be a wife-beater and an attempted murderer. Surely, he'd fooled everyone, until he'd tried to kill Rose in a fit of fury, leaving a mountain of evidence in his wake. Evidence which of course, according to John had been planted and that he'd been framed. *Right.* I wondered if he thought I was sympathetic to his story. I wasn't.

I told him I wanted to interview him because I was researching domestic violence and wanted the perspective of the accused. Seated across from him in the dank room, I looked him in the eyes. "Tell me about yourself."

He sat back with a grin that tilted one cheek and didn't hesitate to go into great detail about how he'd fought his way out of poverty by gaining acceptance to the University of Washington on a full scholarship. He crossed his thick arms. "Upon graduation, I landed an entry-level position at a tech firm and then climbed up the ranks until I made it to the c-suite." He claimed to have been the most successful person in his entire family.

I narrowed my eyes but quickly softened my gaze. "So, you'd say you had a pretty good life up until now?" I asked, keeping the casual conversation going.

Based on Rose's account, it had all been true. I could see how a smart and successful woman like Rose, or any other woman who didn't know the signs of abuse, could've fallen for his charm. Rose had explained that he hadn't been abusive until after they had been married and that it was like a switch had been flipped. She thought she'd married the man of her dreams, only to find out later he was the monster in her nightmares—a master manipulator and textbook narcissist.

"Not just good, *extremely* good. That is until I ended up in here." His titled grin faded into a menacing frown.

His coworkers, friends, and family had insisted he was a wonderful man and explained how they just couldn't believe it was true. Of course, he'd made their life seem perfect on the outside. Rose had been too terrified to let anybody know what it was really like in their home, which she described as a prison. *Karma*, I thought while staring at him and taking a calm breath.

I had to admit, he was superb at playing the victim, but I could play too. My strategy was to use sugar rather than vinegar to get the information I wanted. I needed to throw him off guard by acting sympathetic.

I asked with an expression of grave concern, "So you had absolutely nothing to do with the attempted murder of your wife?"

He shook his head vigorously. "Of course not. I love Rose. I miss her so much. I'd never hurt her. Never. I've only ever tried to protect her. Did you know she's never visited me since I was arrested? Rumor has it she's not even in Seattle anymore."

He seemed to be fishing. I didn't take the bait.

"Have you asked any friends or family or hired someone to check in on her to see how she's doing?"

His dark blue eyes now appeared almost black. His relaxed demeanor and charming disposition shifted to hardness. His true self revealed. "My family and friends are devastated that I'm in here. I only took a plea to spare them and Rose the anguish of a trial, even though I'm innocent. I didn't want to bother them, and unfortunately, the legal fees and the divorce settlement cleaned me out. I'd love to be able to hire a private investigator to find out how she's doing. I'm worried sick about her."

What was intended to sound like a warm sentiment came across to me like ice-cold hatred. This guy thought he had the world fooled, and from the way he spoke to me, he must've thought I was born last week. I hunched over and leaned forward, lowering my voice. "I can only imagine what you're going through."

He raised his hands in defeat and shrugged. "It is what it is. I know once I'm out, I'll be able to reclaim my life. I've built myself from nothing before, and I can do it again. My only concern is for Rose."

He was pretty optimistic for a felon with thirteen years ahead of him. Maybe he'd stashed money away before he was locked up. I wouldn't be surprised. His fake concern for Rose irked me. Time for the curveball.

"That's a noble attitude. Why are you so worried about Rose? Do you think someone is after her?"

He cocked his head. "Did she send you here?"

I remained silent.

He straightened his posture, and his plastic face he was trying to pass off as sympathetic reappeared. "Oh, dear. She has, hasn't she? She must be having one of her episodes." He shook his head.

I raised my brows. "Episodes?"

"I'm afraid Rose has mental health issues. It's why I ended up here. It's why I didn't fight her when she had insisted I attacked her. Poor thing. If she hasn't told you, her father abused both her and her mother. The PTSD caused flashbacks on more than one occasion when she'd mistaken me for her father. I begged her to get the help she needs. I love her so much, but she wouldn't listen. Now, I'm here. All because I fell in love with a troubled woman. So, she sent you? Does she think I've escaped and am after her? Typical delusion, I'm afraid. As you can see, I'm very much locked up." He crossed his arms again.

For the love of all that is holy. A flashback didn't cause bruises. This guy was the delusional one, maybe even a sociopath. I shoved down my disgust and said with a tight-lipped smile, "No, she doesn't think that. She received a strange email and thought maybe you had sent it. Did you?"

His darkness returned. He leaned forward with the devil in his stare. "I'm not allowed email. I'm not allowed more than an hour outside. All because of that psycho bitch. You can tell her I wish I'd finished the job." He spat on the floor and pushed his chair back. He growled, "Guard, we're done here."

A chill shot down my spine, but I didn't flinch. It shouldn't surprise me how quickly he had turned from lukewarm to freezing cold. It must've been what Rose experienced during the three years of their marriage.

John didn't slip or make reference that he'd sent someone after her, but it didn't mean he hadn't. I had no doubt he would go after her when he was on the outside. Once I figured out who was tormenting Rose, she and I would have to discuss future plans. If John Mudgett were free, Rose would never be safe.

On the drive to the airport, I called into the office and requested one of the analysts pull all records for John Mudgett. I wanted financial records and a list of family, friends, and cellmates. Everything. I needed to know who was associating with this guy and doing his dirty work while he was locked up.

Mrs. Pearson asked, "Anything else?"

As I pulled off the highway, I added, "Yeah, give me a list of anybody who's been released from King County Correctional in the last year, along with driver license photos, if possible."

"I'll send the request over right away."

"Anything else?"

"Have we received the fingerprint results for Rose's case yet?"

Mrs. Pearson paused. "Yes, just in. No hits, I'm afraid."

Damn. Though I hadn't been hopeful there would be.

"Anything else?" She asked.

"No. Thank you. Please put a rush on the background."

"Understood. Travel safe."

I approached Seattle-Tacoma airport and sadness cloaked me. I'd visited Seattle with Jared. We both loved the city. Pike Place. The amazing bookstores. The coffee. It must've been gut-wrenching for Rose to have to leave such a great home. I couldn't promise she would ever be able to return safely, but I could promise to catch the bastard who was trying to make her flee once again.

CHAPTER THIRTEEN

MARTINA

Flipping through the pages, I studied the printout of all the prisoners released from King County Correctional over the last year. There were hundreds of names on the list. It would take forever to print out DMV photos.

It was nearly five o'clock on Friday afternoon, and my eyes were glazing over. I needed to get the pictures printed in order for Rose to review them to see if anyone looked familiar. There were just too many names to get through in the allotted time frame. The quicker we could identify who broke into her apartment, the quicker Rose could have her life back.

I glanced up at Will, our latest college intern, approaching my desk. "Hey. Thank you for the list."

"No problem. I came by to let you know Stavros is back and to ask if I could assist you further, ma'am."

Stavros was back. He'd been out of the office for the last two weeks. It would be good to see him and get his take on Roes's case. I eyed Will. Will had taken to the ways of the office pretty quickly. Stavros ran his ship like it was heading to war, drilling into the young ones as if they were Army recruits.

"Maybe. Is there a way to cut it down — make it more manageable?"

Will squinted and nodded. "I could cut it down by date and give you a list based on the month."

"That would be great. How long will it take to rerun it?"

"Give me ten minutes. I'll print it and bring it by before I leave."

"Perfect."

As Will rushed off, I thought, *He'll do okay*.

I hoped to find a person in cahoots with Rose's ex in the list of ex-cons. Hope was the operative word because if it wasn't a known associate of John Mudgett's, it could be anybody. *Anybody* would be a lot more challenging to track down. In the last two days, the surveillance team hadn't picked up on anything unusual in or around Rose's home or office. Nobody appeared to be following her.

If God was smiling on Rose, perhaps the alarm spooked the stalker, and he was backing off. Or maybe he was moving on to his next victim. Maybe Rose was safe, but not the next lady. I wished for Rose's sake that he was moving on and she was free, but I couldn't take that chance. I couldn't lose another one. I just couldn't. Maybe after Rose's case was closed, I'd finally take a break. I was tired of pretending everything was perfect. I needed to recharge and get straight. And Zoey would be over the moon if we took a trip to Disneyland. *The happiest place on Earth.* That sounded perfect.

While waiting for Will to return, I busied myself with emails to avoid thinking about anything else. I'd much rather be sifting through files than being reminded of the fact that a year ago today, my world was blown apart.

"Ma'am"

I looked up at Will. "What have you got?"

He handed me the stack of papers. "I have them stapled by month, with the most recent on top. If there's nothing else ..."

"Thank you, Will. How long will it take to print out DMV photos of each one of these?"

His mouth parted. "Um, I'm not sure."

Noticing the time on my monitor, I waved my hand to dismiss the request. "I'm sorry, I know it's late. You can go. Thank you again." It was nearly five o'clock, and the entire office was supposed to head over to the restaurant to celebrate Jared. Dread sunk in. I'd rather be looking through photos trying to keep Rose safe than have to dredge up the memories slowly breaking me in half.

"It's not a problem. It's just we have the ... I could do it now or I can come in early tomorrow?"

I knew Will was supposed to be off tomorrow. Poor kid. He had plans and a life. I could do it myself and not make the guy suffer. "No, that's okay. I'll take care of it."

"Are you sure? I'm happy to come in tomorrow."

I gave him my best reassuring smile. "No, really, it's fine. I've got it. Thank you and I'll see you at the party."

He nodded and swiftly exited.

He clearly wanted to get away from me as fast as possible. I hadn't intended to make him uncomfortable. Was there anything I didn't ruin? I needed a break. I saw that now. I should've taken a break a year ago but had been too proud. Too frozen. Back then, I wanted to think of anything but what my life would look like from that point forward. I hadn't wanted to face that nothing would ever be the same.

THE SHOT GLASS THUDDED ON THE TABLE—ANOTHER ONE down the hatch, in the name of remembering my dead husband.

Like I could have ever forgotten. The rowdy group fondly shared stories from back in Jared's days in the army. Jared was strong, tough, powerful, but he was funny too. Yes, Jared was wonderful and worthy of celebration. But I felt stuck and unable to get over the loss. Hearing stories didn't comfort me. It was just a terrible reminder of what I no longer had. What Zoey would never know. Her memories would be of six short years. Memories that would fade over time. It was a travesty. With anger bubbling up, I waved over the waiter. "Can I get another?"

A tip of the chin and the waiter hurried off. If you asked me, the waiter couldn't return quick enough. I eyed Stavros's sheepish grin. He knew I was miserable. He knew I didn't want to be here. He knew — somehow — that I was just putting on a face. Stavros had become like family, like an uncle always looking out for me.

His warm eyes met mine. "How are you holding up?"

"I'm all right, I suppose," I lied.

"You seem to have a full mind."

If only I could hide from Stavros, all of my secrets would be safe. "Yes. I feel guilty sitting here when I could be working on Rose's case." I continued on, explaining the current status of the case.

He frowned. "You should be taking care of you, Martina."

How could he say that? He didn't really expect me to abandon Rose or my job? My job and Zoey were all I had left. I had to stay strong, or at least pretend to be until Rose was safe. "I'm taking care of myself. Don't worry. I think maybe I'll head back to the office and do some work before heading home."

Stavros focused his gaze on the empty glasses in front of my place setting. "You sure you're okay to drive?"

I was barely buzzed. I wished I was drunk, a blackout,

forget-everything kind of drunk. "I'm fine." *Four drinks were nothing.*

Stavros looked at me skeptically, although he tried to have a stoic face. I knew he wasn't buying it, but I was suffocating and needed to do something. I couldn't sit here and let them see me spiral out of control. "No, really, I'm fine. Do you mind if I just sneak out? I ..."

He put his massive hand on my shoulder. "Go ahead, I'll cover for you."

I stood up and grabbed my backpack, sliding a strap over my arm. I looked down at his dark, concerned eyes. "Thank you. I'll see you Monday."

Back at the office, I sat at my desk and opened the bottom drawer, where I kept a hidden bottle of Jameson. Ever since Julie, I needed to make sure I had some handy. It was temporary. I would take a vacation soon. I would start back at the cross-fit gym and stock the house with veggies and lean protein. I could beat this. I just needed a momentary reprieve.

I pulled out the bottle of Irish whiskey, fitting considering my Irish exit from the bar, and unscrewed the top, drinking directly from the bottle. My insides burned from my throat to my belly. I felt warm and tingly all over. I replaced the bottle back in my drawer and studied the stack of papers in front of me. I had work to do, and I wasn't going anywhere until I was done printing each one of these jerks' pictures. Tomorrow morning, I'd head over to Rose's and we'd get to the bottom of things.

I mindlessly printed until I had the last three months of released inmate photos ready at the printer. I pushed off from my chair, stumbling after my foot got caught on the leg, but I quickly steadied myself before swaying over to the printer station. Grabbing the stack, I put them in a large envelope and headed back to my desk for one last sip of medicine. Home was calling my name.

CHAPTER FOURTEEN

MARTINA

I GROANED AS A MAN SHOUTED THROUGH THE WINDOW. "Ma'am, are you okay? Ma'am, can you hear me? Ma'am, I need you to open the door."

The yelling was loud, and it hurt my ears. Where am I? Damn, my head throbbed. Why were they shouting? Why were there flickering lights? *Too bright.* I tried to lean back, but my body defied me. The door flung open, and two sets of arms reached for me, pulling me out of my seat. I tried to catch my breath as they lay me on the hard plastic. The shouting was louder. The man yelled again. "Ma'am, can you tell me your name?

I mumbled, "Martina," before I surrendered to sleep once more.

———

I WOKE TO CHILLY, ANTISEPTIC-FILLED AIR WITH fluorescent lighting overhead. I tried to sit up, but it felt like a small child was sitting on top of my chest. Why was I in a hospital? What day was it? My body twitched. Zoey? Who had

Zoey? I had to get to Zoey. I yanked the IV line from my arm and ripped the tubes from my nostrils. I sat up, and the pain shot through my back, halting my escape. What the hell had happened? Why was I here? I searched the bed for the call buttons.

A few minutes later, a man with blue scrubs and sun-kissed skin rushed toward me. "You're awake." He eyed my IV line. "Oh dear, what have you done-"

"Where's my daughter? Where's Zoey? Who has Zoey?" I snapped.

He said, "Your daughter isn't here. I need you to lay back. Did you take out your IV?"

Through gritted teeth, I growled. "I need to get to my daughter."

"You need to calm down. You aren't going anywhere in your condition. You were in a car accident. You have broken ribs and a concussion. Now I need to put your line back in and call the doctor. Honey, you're no good to anyone if you're dead."

Dramatic much? I layed back on the bed. "Fine. Where's my phone?"

He pushed buttons on the IV machine. Without looking, he said, "Not sure. You can make local calls with the bedside phone. Now, stay put, and I'll be right back with a new kit."

I stretched out my arm to reach the phone. I winced. It felt like I'd been stabbed in the chest. I took a few deep breaths before dialing Claire's number. "Hi, It's Martina. Do you have Zoey?"

"No. Oh my god. Is she missing?"

Panic rose and then fell. *Damn.* I forgot she was at Kaylie's for the sleepover. "No, no. Sorry, I forgot she had a sleepover. I had an accident last night, and I'm in the hospital. I couldn't remember where she was. I'm going to call over to Kaylie's."

"Oh my god! Are you okay?"

"I'll be fine. I'm sorry to have disturbed you."

"Are you being discharged soon? Do you need me to pick up Zoey and stay with her at the house?"

Shoot. I had no idea when I would be released. "Maybe. I'll call over to Kaylie's and then call you back, okay?"

"No problem. Anything you need. Don't hesitate to call me."

I thanked her and hung up the phone. *Damn.* I didn't know Kaylie's number by heart. Where were my things? I redialed Claire.

"I'm sorry, Claire, it's Martina again. I just realized I don't have my phone or purse and don't know Kaylie's number. Would you do me a huge favor and go over to Kaylie's — she's just down the block."

"I know where she lives."

"Yes, please pick up Zoey and call me when you get to my house?"

"No problem. I'll leave now."

"Thank you, Claire."

I sighed with relief. I'd exhale completely when I heard Zoey's voice.

A flash of last night sprinted across my mind. The photo IDs. Rose. Where were the printouts? I needed Rose to see them.

The nurse returned with a chipper tone. "Okay, let's get you all hooked up." He opened the package and wiped the back of my hand with an alcohol swab. "Did you find your daughter?"

"Yes, she's at a friend's house. Do you, uh, know what happened — the accident, I mean?" I was afraid to hear the answer.

"From what I understand, you rammed your car into a telephone pole on the side of the highway."

"Were there any other cars involved?"

"No."

I exhaled. *Thank God.* What had I done?

"All righty, you're all set. How's your pain level?"

"It's fine," I said before pain contorted my face. Pain I deserved.

"Are you sure? You look like you're struggling? How about I give you a bit more to make you comfortable. Is that okay?"

I nodded.

He stepped in front of the IV pump and pushed a few buttons. "Okay. You're all set. I'll get the doctor in to talk to you."

"Thanks."

I watched as the nurse exited the room. Out of sight, I broke down. It all came flooding back to me. The bar. The whiskey. Jared. Flickering lights. I had thought I'd seen Jared. It wasn't Jared. It was a telephone pole. How could I have been so careless?

My body froze at the sound of the telephone ring. Zoey. I grimaced as I reached for the phone. Before I spoke, I wiped my tear-streaked face with the back of my hand. "Zoey!"

Zoey screeched into the phone. "Mommy!"

I shut my eyes as the tears threatened to escape once again. "Hi, honey. How are you?"

"I'm great. Kaylie's mom painted our nails and braided my hair. It looks terrific."

I exhaled. Zoey was fine. My baby was okay.

I felt the blood drain from my face; I came too close to never seeing Zoey again. Zoey would've been an orphan. The thought rattled me to the core. I swallowed in the sob that threatened to escape. "Sounds great. I can't wait to see it."

"When are you coming home?"

My eyelids became heavy, as my head entered into a fog. The meds. "Soon. Claire will stay with you until I'm home."

"Okay. Love you, Mommy!"

"I love you too, baby. Let me talk to Claire, okay?"

Focusing was difficult, but I managed to tell Claire I'd call her later and assure her everything would be fine. She deserved a raise. And a bonus. Hanging up the phone, a wave of warmth flushed through me. I didn't deserve to sleep, but I didn't have the power to stop it.

STAVROS, A HULK OF A MAN, APPROACHED MY HOSPITAL bed, shaking his head. *Crap.* "Stavros. I was just about to call. How did you know?" He was ex-special forces turned private security-he had his ways. How had I thought he wouldn't find out?

"What the hell, Martina? I've been covering for you for months. You could've killed yourself or someone else. This crap needs to stop."

My heart pounded in my chest. "I know. I will, I just ..."

He crossed his muscled arms across his bulky chest. "Don't you get it? Zoey wouldn't be able to handle losing you, too. You could lose your PI license. You could lose everything. And, you put the company at risk. This is seriously messed up, Martina. You're out of control, and I'm done covering for you. Effective immediately, you're on leave from work. You won't be permitted back until you've completed a rehab program of my choice, and you're ninety days sober. Before leaving the hospital, Heather will stop by for you to transition all of your open cases to her."

What about Rose? No! "But —"

"This isn't open for discussion. Those are the terms. Make no mistake; if you weren't Jared's wife, you'd be fired. So, your next step is to say thank you, Stavros, and promise you'll get your act together."

Very little got past Stavros, but I had no idea he'd been covering for me, or that he needed to. I was weak. Defeated. Broken.

Nothing he'd said was wrong. Any other boss would've fired me a long time ago. I was just so tired. Tired of the sleepless nights. Tired of missing Jared. Tired of having to do it all alone.

I brushed my hair out of my face and met his gaze. "Thank you, Stavros. I will do the program — whatever you want."

He sighed and his face softened. "It's not about what I want. You need to get sober for your daughter and for your job. I know Jared's death hit you hard; it hit all of us. He was a great guy, but you still have something to live for. You have that little girl of yours. That is who you should do this for. And, the cops know you'd been drinking. You may be facing DUI charges — it'll help your case if you're in a program. So, as soon as you're released, we'll get you into one."

Shame filled me to the core. I wasn't out of the woods yet, I could still lose everything, and I only had myself to blame. I nodded. "They said I should be able to go home tomorrow."

"I'll have Mrs. Pearson work on the arrangements." He unfolded his arms and placed a gentle hand on my arm. "You're one of our best. One of our family. We want you back, so you need to take this time to get well. Take care, Martina."

I tipped my chin and held back the tears as he exited. With Stavros out of eyesight, the flood gates poured open again. As I sobbed quietly in my lonely hospital room, I realized that this was it. I'd hit rock bottom.

CHAPTER FIFTEEN

ROSE

I SQUEEZED THE TRIGGER, AND MY FEET STAGGERED BACK AS my arms bucked from the recoil. Martina wasn't kidding. Firing a gun *would* change my life. I turned to the right to look at my instructor. "Nice. Now do it again," he said.

I refocused on the faceless target, this time widening my stance more. I'd never fired a gun before today, but I wanted to be ready to protect myself. No more running. No more being afraid of my own shadow. Me, Rose Green, would be a strong, lean, fighting machine. Ha. That was my goal, anyway.

After my all-day self-defense training with Martina and my first training at the Krav Maga studio near my apartment, I dared someone to mess with me. As I completed the grueling work to prepare for such an attack, I imagined the look on John's face if he were to come at me again. He'd have that same sick, twisted look in his eye, but then it would shift to one of shock and fear as I proceeded to kick his ass.

After I'd emptied the round in my gun, I set it down on the counter as instructed. In a short amount of time, I was already feeling more confident and less afraid.

I took off the noise-canceling headphones and placed them next to the gun. My hands smelled of steel and gunpowder. "How did I do?" I asked the instructor, who wasn't much taller than me.

"For a first-timer, you're pretty damn good. Maybe even a natural. Well done."

I was proud of myself for finding the courage to take control of my life and for being able to hit a target squarely on the forehead. Sure, I needed to practice and then practice some more, but I could feel the shift in my destiny as I held the heavy metal in my hand. I beamed up at him, "Thank you."

He led me back over to the counter to return the rented pistol and schedule my next lesson. I didn't want to buy my own gun until I felt more confident in my abilities. Soon.

"I'll see you on Tuesday," I said and waved.

Heading out to the parking lot, I stopped when a familiar voice from behind said, "Rose, is that you?"

I swiveled around.

The Texan stood with a wide grin and a pair of brown cowboy boots.

I tried on a friendly smile. "Yes, you're Todd, right?"

"That's right. I didn't know you shoot." He said with his Texas twang. It was kind of sexy. How could I even think of a romantic partner? After John, I had sworn off men, but there was something about Todd. Maybe it was the accent? I'd always been a sucker for a Texas accent.

"Actually, today was my first lesson."

"You don't say? Well, how did you like it?" He asked with kind eyes.

I loved it. It made me feel powerful and in control. "I liked it."

"That's great. More women should know how to protect themselves."

A predator wouldn't say that, right? Not all men were bad, isn't that what my therapist said?

I nodded, unsure of what else to say.

"I just finished up practice and was about to search for sustenance. Maybe try out one of those spots downtown. I hope you don't find me too forward, but would you care to join me? I hate eating alone."

"Umm. Let me check something real quick." I pulled my phone from my purse. Still no call back from Martina. She'd left a message late Friday night saying she wanted to meet yesterday to go over some photos of potential stalkers. I'd called a few times yesterday and this morning, but nothing. She'd been especially attentive since the break-in, and it wasn't like her not to pick up. Maybe Martina was busy with her daughter? *Maybe I'll try one more time before answering Todd.* "I was supposed to meet a friend, but I haven't been able to get a hold of her. Let me call her again. I'd hate to miss her. Do you mind?"

"Not at all, darlin'. Take your time."

Darlin'. The word made her stomach flutter. I really should ease up on the cowboy romance novels. "Thanks."

Facing away from Todd, I dialed Martina and held the phone to my ear. It rang three times before going to voicemail. I shifted on my feet. Was something wrong? I slid the phone back in my purse and turned around, hoping she'd return my call soon. "She still didn't answer."

His minty eyes with flecks of gold twinkled in the sunlight. "Sounds like it's my lucky day. Lunch?"

I cleared my throat, giving myself a second to think. It's not like I'd be riding with him; I'd brought my own car. And, we would be going to a public place. I think Martina would approve. "Sure, why not?" I smiled.

"Great. I was thinking of trying that cantina everyone raves about."

"I've been. It's good. I'll meet you there."

"Yes, ma'am."

As I passed him, I caught a whiff of his spicy cologne. *Yummy*. My life was definitely turning itself right around.

CHAPTER SIXTEEN

MARTINA

THE DOORBELL RANG AND ZOEY BOLTED FOR THE DOOR. I yelled out to her, "Zoey, you know you're not allowed to answer the door by yourself. I'll get it."

Zoey ran back to me in the kitchen and smirked. "I *know*." She exaggerated the last word like I'd been foolish to think she'd be so dense. When had my seven-year-old turned into a teenager?

Zoey flipped her hair and said, "I was just looking to see who it was," and dramatically pursed her lips.

I didn't know what to make of this newfound attitude. She couldn't even reach the peephole, and she knew it. Ever since I'd come home from the hospital yesterday, she'd been acting off. It was as if her bubbly sparkly self took a vacation, paving way to this budding teenager. She'd insisted that not only could she take care of herself, but she was there to take care of me too while I healed from the accident.

After she'd made her declaration, I'd reiterated I was fine, with just a few cracked ribs and a bruise here and there. Zoey wasn't having it. It was as if she understood that the car wreck hadn't destroyed me physically, but mentally, I was in bad shape.

Earlier that morning at my first session of AA, I was taught that it was time to be honest with myself. I *was* in bad shape. Why was it that when you're crashing down, you don't realize it until you've hit the very bottom?

That's exactly where I was. When I'd sat in that uncomfortable plastic chair in the multi-purpose room of the local church that morning, my perspective shifted unexpectedly. The people around the room, my fellow addicts, were what I would've called lowlifes and losers. The pieces of humanity that were bringing us all down. And then they spoke. 90 days sober. 180 days. Ten years. I was the only first-timer. They weren't the losers and lowlifes — I was. I had thought my self-medication was temporary and something I could control, but as I listened to their stories, they were the same stories I'd told myself. I was an addict.

My name is Martina Monroe and I'm an alcoholic.

I was reminded of the old adage: "you can't judge a book by its cover." If all the brave folks who'd spoken up during the meeting hadn't convinced me, Rocco did. Rocco, the heavily tattooed and ex-Hells Angels gang member was ten years sober *and* my AA sponsor. He shared with me his journey from felon to finding God and sobriety. He was the man tasked with helping me get my life on a sober and righteous path. I couldn't think of anyone more fitting. He was compassionate, caring, and tough. Tough on himself, and he'd promised to be tough with me too when I needed it. I'd like to think if Jared were here, they would've been fast friends.

My nerves rattled as I approached the door. I opened it and stood back. "Hey."

Stavros studied me from head to toe. "You look better."

"Thanks, come on in."

He carried in a paper bag and my backpack — my personal effects from the car I wrecked. The vehicle was totaled, and according to those at the scene, I was lucky that I hadn't been.

When I had cried alone in my hospital bed, I wondered if that would have been better. Emotional scars ran a lot deeper than physical ones. But I know that I couldn't think that way. It was wrong and the easy way out. I needed to be here for Zoey.

In the hall, I said, "You didn't have to bring it out here; you could have sent it."

He stopped and turned to me. "I wanted to see how you were doing. Two birds."

He was cut off at the sound of Zoey shrieking, "Uncle Stavros! Uncle Stavros!" She wrapped her tiny arms around his bulky body.

He bent down to accept her warm greeting. "It's good to see you. How are you doing?"

"Good. Claire is here too, which is nice. She's here to help out, since, you know, Mom isn't a 100 percent yet."

Yes. Zoey was seven going on seventeen. Lord, help me.

He straightened out to meet my gaze. "I'm glad to hear you have some help, Martina."

"Are you staying for dinner, Uncle Stavros? Mom just agreed to order pizza and maybe even soda."

I was weak. I didn't usually give her soda because it hyped her up a little more than I could handle, but my guilt got the best of me. I'd almost made her an orphan. She could have soda one night.

"I can't stay. I just want to talk to your mom for a few minutes. Is it okay if we talk by ourselves?"

Zoey frowned but nodded her head and ran off toward the family room where Claire had been setting up an art project to keep her busy. Claire had been a godsend, offering to help with cleaning, grocery shopping, and cooking. I insisted I could do all of it, but I was overruled by both a seven-year-old and her babysitter. Like Rocco had insisted, I had to learn to accept help when it was offered, so I did. And it felt good. Like a weight had been lifted from my whole body.

I didn't know what Stavros wanted to talk to me about, but I couldn't imagine it would be good news.

I ushered him into the dining room and leaned against the contemporary, unfinished wood table. Jared and I had picked out the set shortly after we'd moved into our house. I studied Stavros as he set my belongings down on top of it. Apparently, he'd used up all his smiles and cheery attitude on Zoey. "What did you want to talk to me about? Is it Rose Green's case? Is she okay?"

He answered as if I hadn't said a word. "Have you gone to your first meeting?"

I knew he hadn't been kidding about checking up on me and ensuring that I was doing the program, but I hadn't realized he would be there within twenty-four hours. "Yes, I went this morning." I really hated being watched like a naughty child. I didn't like it, but I supposed I deserved it.

"Where's your chip?"

It felt like I'd taken a kick to the chest. *Stavros no longer trusted me.* I couldn't blame him, but that didn't mean it didn't hurt. I fished the silver token out of my pocket and held it up.

He tipped his chin. "Good. Do you have a sponsor?"

"Yes, his name is Rocco. Ten years sober. Ex-Hells Angel, if you can believe that."

A slight grin crept on one side of his chiseled face. "Good. You need someone tough."

Stavros was rarely wrong, and this was no exception.

"How are things at the office? Who's handling Rose's case?"

The smile faded. "Heather is. She told me she'd reach out to Rose today and let her know there's been a change and that you're no longer on duty due to medical reasons. You don't need to worry about Rose or anybody at the office. All you need to worry about is getting better and stronger and being the best version of you. When you're better, we'll talk about reinstating you."

Shameful emotions bubbled up inside of me. I was lucky to have Stavros for a boss, a boss that cared about my daughter and me. The firm really was a family. I suppressed the tears. "Thank you, Stavros, for everything."

He tapped his hand on the table. "Glad to hear you're on track and doing better. I'll be checking in. I need to head out now, but I'll say a quick goodbye to Zoey and be outa your hair."

I was frozen as he exited. I didn't want him to see me break down, and I feared if I moved, the dam would break.

———

I WASHED MY FACE BEFORE HEADING BACK INTO THE dining room to retrieve my things and bring them into the kitchen. I pulled out my work cell phone from my backpack. Dead. I plugged it in to the charger that was already dangling from the electrical outlet. The screen illuminated. Seven missed calls. I was on strict orders not to answer, but once it was charged, I'd check the messages, just in case there was important information I needed to relay to Heather.

I pulled the stack of papers out and put them on the dining table. The messy stack of papers were photos I had planned to bring over to Rose. Frustration flared within me. It was my job to protect Rose. She needed to look at these right away. Two days ago to be exact. Damn. I was dying to know how she was doing, but I couldn't risk losing my job. Surely if something had gone wrong, I would've heard about it.

Either way, I needed to call the office to make sure the

photos were taken to Rose. Before I could straighten the stack, Zoey ran into the kitchen at full speed, with pink paint on her fingertips. "Mommy, Mommy, we're finger painting. Do you want to join us?"

Usually, I would've been afraid she'd get paint on the tile, but her wide eyes and excitement were a sight for sore eyes. It was far better than the snotty teen act.

She continued flailing her arms around, dancing as children often did for no particular reason. "Sure, give me a second, and I'll be right in."

"Yeah!" She flung herself around, twirling, causing the stack of papers to scatter, some landing on the ground. She stopped with a frown. "Sorry, Mommy. I can help clean up."

I gave her a reassuring smile. "No, that's okay, honey. Go back into the family room, and I'll join you in a minute."

She agreed and skittered out. I could hear her calling out to Claire, "Mommy's coming!"

I shook my head with a smile on my face. I knelt to pick up the papers, and my heart stopped.

It couldn't be.

Staring back at me on the page was Rose's neighbor, Todd. The hair color was darker, but that face was the same. It was undeniable. Rose was in danger.

With the printout of Todd's face in hand, I picked up my cell phone still attached to the charger. All of the missed calls were from Rose.

My heart thudded so loud, it pulsed in my ears.

I listened to her messages, and a tiny bit of relief entered me. Rose had been inquiring about the missed appointment, not of any incidents with her stalker. *With Todd.* I knew it was against the rules of my probation, but I had to call. If I lost my job for defying orders, so be it. I couldn't let anything happen to Rose.

CHAPTER SEVENTEEN

ROSE

"Who was that, darlin'?" Todd asked with that adorable Southern accent of his. Ever since lunch yesterday, I couldn't stop thinking about him. He was sweet and strong—a real gentleman. I was excited when he'd knocked on my door after work and asked if I wanted to go out to dinner. I was already boiling pasta, so I'd offered a home-cooked meal instead.

He was certainly a pleasant distraction from recent events. Things were definitely turning around. I hadn't even gotten any creepy stalker notes or any other signs of the stalker since the break-in. Maybe the stalker had given up once he saw me around town with a burly, strong man. Perhaps Todd had scared him off. Wouldn't that be something?

I locked the door behind me and headed back to the dining table. "A friend of mine, who asked I meet with her after we were done with dinner. I hope you don't mind. We're supposed to have met this past weekend, but she was in an accident, she's feeling better and has asked me to meet her at her office."

He tilted his head and jutted his chin, as if skeptical. "At her office? Doesn't sound very social."

I slid into my seat and picked up my glass of red wine.

Martina had told me not to tell anyone anything about the case. Her cover was that of a real estate agent. I thought it was a bit overcautious but figured it wouldn't hurt either. "She's a real estate agent, and she's helping me find a place to buy."

"I didn't know you were thinking of moving?"

Could he tell I was lying? "I'm not fond of apartment living or being a renter, and it would be nice to own a house." All true.

"That's a great idea. Are you looking somewhere outside of Pleasant Ridge? I was under the impression it was a safe neighborhood, but I see all the extra locks on your front door. Maybe I was wrong?"

Was it odd that he asked about my extra security? Martina had warned me to question everything when meeting with new people, and people I didn't know very well. But he was my neighbor. What were the odds that my neighbor was my stalker? Unlikely, right? Plus, Todd seemed like a catch, not someone who needed to stalk someone for companionship. I shrugged the cautious notion off. "No, it's a safe place. I blame my single gal paranoia."

Kind of.

"Really? I thought I heard the police here the other morning?"

My body went rigid. "Oh, that. I thought I had an intruder, but the cops think I forgot to lock the door and that the wind blew it open. It's silly when I think about it now." The wriggling in my gut made me realize I didn't know this man at all. How had I been so careless? I attempted to hide my panic with a chuckle.

Todd set his empty wine glass down. "Well, it sounds like you need to get to a meeting with your real estate agent friend. Too bad, I was hoping we could watch a movie and spend some more time together. What's the urgency, anyhow? Surely, you're not looking at houses tonight?" His tone was accusatory.

My pulse quickened, and suddenly it was hot in my apartment. "Oh, it's not urgent, she's just been through a lot, and it sounds like she needs someone to talk to. We've gotten closer since we started working together."

He stood up. "Is that so? I kind of get the feelin' it's something else. Are you seeing another man?"

What?

I glanced up at Todd. His pupils widened under the lowlights, making his kind eyes darken.

Damn it. My taser was in my purse—in the bedroom closet.

"No, nothing like that."

He moved closer, looming over me. "You're hiding something. What is it, Rose?"

I could knee him. That would be the most effective. "Nothing. I don't like your tone. You should leave now." My voice quivered.

I winced as he bent down and whispered in my ear. "Rose, I'm not going anywhere."

I shifted my knee toward his groin, but he caught it and chuckled. "I can tell you like me. I like you. There's no reason to be afraid or act like that."

His tone sent chills down my spine. "What happened to your accent?"

He bellowed a hearty laugh as he blocked my escape with his body. "Oh honey, I'm from Washington, not Texas, but when I saw your library of cowboy books, I knew you couldn't resist."

My heart sunk. It was Todd. This whole time. Oh, this was bad, very bad. I was no match for Todd. I needed to get my Taser. I glanced over my shoulder toward my bedroom, then back at my front door. *I could try to make a run for it.* It wouldn't work. "You were right. I like you."

He stepped back. "Then why are you trying to hurt me? *I* don't want to hurt *you*."

I shook my head and anxiously giggled. "It's my paranoia. I'm so sorry. Can we maybe start over?"

Had he bought it?

He paced as he seemed to contemplate my proposition.

Twiddling his fingers, he stopped and eyed me. "I like that idea. How about that movie? Netflix is full of them. Why don't you join me on the couch, where we can get a little closer?"

The suggestion made my skin crawl. "Sounds good. Would you like more wine?"

All objects were potential weapons.

"No, I think I'm good."

He grabbed my hand and led me to the sofa. I tried my breathing exercises to calm my nerves. One, to think clearly, and two, so he wouldn't be set off. I slowly sat down on the couch. I could feel his eyes burning into me. Perhaps he was skeptical of the new act and was making sure I didn't make any sudden moves.

He sat next to me and put his arm around my shoulders. "Now that's better, isn't it?"

No, not at all. "Yes"

"You know I wanted to be close to you for a long time."

Long time? "Is that so?"

"Yes, I admit, I've been watching you for a while," he said with a creepy cheer in his voice, as if I'd find it flattering.

"I don't understand. You're from Washington. Did John send you?"

"John, no, no, no, darlin'."

"So you don't know my ex-husband, John?"

"I did know your ex-husband, but he didn't send me. We were bunked together for a while. Oh, how he talked about you. I knew I had to see you for myself. He was right — you are beautiful. In a way, I'm thankful for him, because he brought us together."

Todd, or whatever his name, was deranged with a capital D. If I didn't fight back, it would end very badly for me. I gathered all my courage and made a fist with my thumbs protruding. *Eyes. Groin. Run.*

I shot my thumbs out toward his eyes, but he was too fast. He grabbed my hands and shoved me to the ground, straddling me. He laughed. "Oh, no, no, darlin', there's no need for that. But just in case you get inclined to do so again, I got something for you."

From his back pocket, he pulled out a bundle of nylon rope and tied my wrists together. I pleaded. "You don't have to do this, you know. I won't try it again. I promise we can just talk or watch a movie like we planned."

I knew that we wouldn't be doing anything as planned.

He glared down at me. "I'd love to believe you, but I can't. Don't worry, you'll love it. I promise."

It? I didn't like the sound of that.

He tightened the ropes, and my wrists burned. I flinched away from him.

He leaned over me and stared into my eyes. "I've been waiting for you for a long time, Rose." He inched closer and sniffed my neck.

It took everything in me not to throw up the pasta primavera and merlot we'd just consumed. When he sat back, he said, "You smell so good," and then he traced his finger down the side of my face.

I recoiled.

He grinned, "Oh no, darlin', you'll like it. Trust me."

New plan. Surely one of the neighbors would hear. I opened my mouth to scream, but it all went black.

CHAPTER EIGHTEEN

MARTINA

Adrenaline pumping, I ran into the living room. Zoey intently painted what looked like a flower and giggled alongside her sitter. "Claire, I need to run out. Will you stay with Zoey?"

"Of course."

Zoey pouted her lips. "You said you'd paint with us."

I hated disappointing Zoey, but this was life or death, I could paint another time. "Sorry, honey, it's an emergency."

"I thought you didn't have to work."

"This is different, I'll explain later, but I have to go." I waved as I rushed to my room. I couldn't bear to look at Zoey's disappointed face right now, and I had to get to Rose.

After unlocking the gun safe in my closet, I slipped on my arm holster and loaded the gun inside. I threw on a jacket to not alarm anyone and to conceal it from Todd. According to his rap sheet, he was a felon who was convicted for a violent sexual assault and did time with Rose's ex. I didn't know if he was working for Mudgett or had his own agenda. Either way, I had to stop him.

I quickly exited my room and hit the front door when I realized I didn't have my cell phone. Not that I had a charger in my rental car, but I needed to call Stavros. I headed back into the kitchen with my ribs on fire. Grabbing the cell, I dialed Stavros. Shoot. Straight to voicemail. I left a message, with all pertinent details like the felon's name and Rose's address, before reaching up into the cabinet for a handful of Ibuprofen. I washed the little miracle pills down with a cup of water that was on the countertop.

I ran-limped out of the house and climbed into my economy-sized rental car. The tires squealed as I tore out of the driveway and headed toward the highway. While driving, I prayed Stavros wouldn't fire me. Surely he had to understand the danger Rose was in. By the time I waited for a callback and a team on the ground, it could be too late. In these situations, minutes could be the difference between whether someone lived or died, or worse.

I contemplated dialing the police, but if Todd hadn't turned on her yet, it would look like a false alarm. Too many of those and the police wouldn't take a real threat seriously.

Maybe I should call Rose on the way to check on her? Not that I could get there any faster if she weren't all right. Plus, calling to check on her five minutes after our last conversation might set off alarm bells. I hadn't wanted her to panic so I'd told her to meet me at the office. If she started acting funny, it could set Todd off and make him escalate, if he hadn't already. I checked the cell phone screen—7 percent battery. I couldn't risk using up all the battery on a welfare check.

On a good day, I could take this guy on my own, but my ribs burned. Sweat dripped down my back, and my pits were soaked through the blazer. I needed the Ibuprofen to kick in fast.

I reached the exit to Rose's apartment, raced through the traffic-free streets, and turned into her complex. Luck was on our side today. I stepped one foot out of my car when the cell phone buzzed. Thank God. "Hey Stavros, I just got here."

"I need you to stay in your car and call 9-1-1. Wait for backup."

I shook my head to nobody in general. "There may not be time. She's with him right now, alone in her apartment. He's already broken into her house once while she was there, knowing she was home. She's in danger, Stavros. I can't in good conscience just sit here and wait for backup."

A heavy sigh sounded through the earpiece. Stavros said, "Call the police. I'm on my way." The line went dead.

There was no way I was waiting for assistance. I held my side and rushed up the stairs to Rose's second-floor apartment. I exhaled coolly, trying to calm myself before knocking. Sweat trickled down my temples.

I rapped my knuckles on Rose's doors. No answer. No sound of footsteps approaching. I studied my surroundings and took the cell from my pocket—4 percent battery. I dialed Rose's number, but it went to voicemail. I shook off the sinking feeling in my stomach and quickly dialed 9-1-1 and pulled out the gun from my holster.

"9-1-1, what's your emergency?"

Without answering, I set the phone on the ground and eyed the door. At full strength, I could break it down — maybe I still could. I took a deep breath and shot out my boot heel to kick at the door jam. Despite the adrenaline, searing pain shot through me, and I cried out. Once steadied, I yelled out, "Rose!"

I received no response and entered. The living room was empty, but Rose's sofa cushions were askew. Not good. I headed toward her bedroom and was met by Todd's devilish stare. I raised my weapon. "Don't come any closer or I'll shoot!"

He stopped in his tracks with his hands raised. I didn't want to shoot him, but I would absolutely shoot him in the face if he moved an inch. Ignoring the pain coursing through my body, I asked, "Where's Rose?"

"Wow. No need for guns. It's me, Todd, Rose's neighbor. Don't you remember? I'm only here to help with a leaky faucet. Rose is out right now."

Right. I tightened the grip on my gun. "Oh, I know exactly who you are, *Michael.* I'll ask one more time. Where is Rose?"

I could hear the static of the 9-1-1 operator trying to understand what was happening. I yelled out Rose's address and the message to come quickly. Todd took a stepped toward me.

I usually could physically fight him, but between the running and kicking down the door, the gun was my only option to defeat him. I aimed the gun at Todd-Michael's face and stared into his eyes. "Where is Rose?"

In a flicker, he lunged, and I squeezed the trigger three times before letting up. His body dropped to the floor with a thud. Blood began to seep beneath him. I studied his motionless chest. I didn't want to risk checking for a pulse.

Heading to the bedroom, I spotted Rose on the bed with her wrists tied together. Her eyes fluttered as she began waking up. She had the start of a black eye and a fat lip. He must've knocked her out. I untied her and then wrapped my arms around her as she cried. She leaned back, sobbing, "It happened so fast. It was Todd, it was always Todd."

She'd have some new scars, but at least she was safe. "I know. I promise he'll never hurt you again."

"How can you?"

"He's dead."

Her eyes widened and the tears stopped. "What? Are you sure?"

"He came after me and I shot him. He's not breathing. Police should be on their way." Remembering my low battery, I asked, "Where's your phone?"

"It was in the kitchen."

"Okay, stay here." I hurried back to the kitchen, grabbed the phone, and looked at the dead body. If I'd been any later, he would've done heinous things to Rose. I dialed Stavros and told him about the situation. He told me he'd deal with me later, but that he was about twenty minutes out.

I didn't regret defying his order. If I hadn't been in the accident, none of this would've happened. If I'd been more reliable, Rose would've been safer. My body shook and tears streamed down my face. I shook my head, and the teardrops splashed onto the linoleum.

Rose approached the dining room and stopped in the doorway. Her gaze rested on Todd's lifeless body.

I wiped my cheeks. "Rose, why don't you go back inside your room until the police get here."

Without moving a muscle, she said, "He's really dead."

I walked over to her. "I'm so sorry I wasn't here sooner."

She turned to face me. "How did you know?"

I ushered her back into the bedroom and explained the photos, the reason I had for not telling her I was coming over, and everything I knew about Todd, including his real name, Michael W. Pierce. In turn, she explained all the gory details of what Todd-Michael had said to her and what he had planned to do with her. He was a sick man, and I was glad he was gone forever. My heart broke for Rose, but I was glad she was safe — at least for now.

CHAPTER NINETEEN

MARTINA

I WALKED APPREHENSIVELY TOWARD MRS. PEARSON. How much did she know? If I were a betting woman, I would have guessed she knew everything. The pursed magenta lips and tipped brow nearly confirmed it. It was the look of pity — my least favorite way to be greeted. It was the face that so many had given me after Jared's death.

I couldn't muster an expression beyond that of defeat. No booze meant no candy-coated feelings. This was me: raw, sober, and a little defeated. "Hi, Mrs. Pearson."

Instead of her typical polite acknowledgment, she stood up and embraced me in a tight squeeze. The scent of her lavender and vanilla perfume filled my senses and sent me back to the first time she'd hugged me after Jared died. Why did everything have to remind me of him? I gently patted her right shoulder before she released me.

Mrs. Pearson shifted backward. "How are you, dear?"

"Surviving."

I hoped this wasn't my last time in the office. The job I loved. Working with people who had become my family. Originally, Stavros had mandated a ninety days sober before I could return to work, but since the incident with Rose, he'd said he'd re-evaluate my status at the company after ninety days. He had been angry about me defying orders, but he was glad that the situation turned out okay; it was the only reason he allowed me to close up the case before being put on leave indefinitely. Indefinitely. I hated that word. I hated not knowing what was coming next or if I'd have a job in six months. I hated that I had to go to AA every day. I hated that I craved alcohol from the time I woke up until the time I fell asleep. Yeah, I was angry. Angry at myself. I knew that I deserved all I received.

Mrs. Pearson's faced softened. "We're all hoping for a healthy and long-lasting recovery for you."

I mumbled, "Thank you," before heading back to the conference room that I had been assured was ready for us.

When I entered the small conference room, my old laptop sat on the table, along with two bottles of water. Since I'd failed to follow orders, as Stavros put it, he'd insisted I return all of my company-issued equipment. My laptop. My cell phone. Everything that connected me to the workplace.

My hands shook as I opened the lid to my computer. I studied the screen and the only icon was a folder labeled: Rose Green Case Files. The rest of my digital folders were gone. Another punch to the gut. They didn't even trust me with my files. I supposed I deserved that.

I clicked through to the report named Michael W. Pierce. As I read the background intel detailed in the report, I still wasn't sorry he was dead. In my humble opinion, he was beyond reform, and it was him or me. I chose me.

A rap on the door drew my attention from the lengthy file to the entrance of the room. There stood Rose, looking more like her old self and wearing a pencil skirt and a fuchsia blouse paired with a colorful, chunky necklace. The only thing out of place were the bruises on her face, now subtle shades of yellows and greens beneath her makeup. I propped myself up and extended my hand. "Good to see you, Rose."

She glanced down at my hand and ignored it, opting for a light embrace instead. She whispered, "Thank you, Martina."

I studied her face. Her eyes, despite her trauma, had a ray of light in them. It was good to see. My insides warmed, knowing she was safe and what appeared to be thriving. Taking a seat, I said, "All in a day's work. How are you feeling?"

She took the hint and sat across from me, dropping her bag onto the carpet. In a chipper tone, she explained, "I'm doing well. In the last few days, I've come to a lot of realizations about myself, about my life, and about what I want. I'm not letting this incident scare me off from living. I'll definitely be more careful of seemingly handsome strangers, but even though I don't know exactly what the future brings, I know it won't involve me hiding out. You not only saved my life, but you taught me how to take back control. I don't know how I could ever thank you enough."

I didn't think I deserved all of that, but it meant a lot. "That's great. Are you hitting the gym?"

She chuckled. "Yes, definitely. I'm continuing with the self-defense courses, and I've really upped my game at the gym. Daily workouts have been empowering. I'm also keeping up with the firearm training. I don't want to be afraid ever again."

I liked Rose; she was a survivor. "I'm happy to hear that." If I was never allowed back into the offices of Drakos Security & Investigations, saving Rose would've been worth it. Rose and others like her were why I did this job. If Stavros wouldn't take me back, I'd find another firm. I wasn't giving up. Despite my anger and feelings of defeat, like Rose, I wanted to live my life. I wanted to be by Zoey's side as she grew up and blossomed into an adult. I wanted to get back to work. I wanted to be happy. I hadn't backed down from a challenge before, and I couldn't start now.

I shifted my focus to the screen. "Why I brought you down here was to let you know your case is being closed. I wanted to go over with you what we found out about Todd, aka Michael W. Pierce, if you're interested, and to have a discussion about the future. A thorough investigation was completed into his background, and your ex-husband was re-interviewed." I paused to reflect on my own part in the case. I'd given what felt like endless statements to justify my shooting of Todd-Michael. The detective said it was likely they'd drop the case against me since he'd said it was self-defense. Still, it had been hectic. One potential murder charge down, one DUI charge to go.

Rose's demeanor shifted to a sober tone. "All I want to know is if he was working with John. Todd, uh, Michael said he wasn't."

"Based on the report, Michael W. Pierce wasn't working in coordination with your husband. He had been one of John's cellmates, and apparently, the two of them discussed you at length. What we can piece together is that he became obsessed with you during that time and decided to seek you out."

Rose's eyes pleaded with me. "You're sure my ex had nothing to do with this?"

"My team seemed fairly certain, but there's always a slight possibility, but it's unlikely."

Rose smirked with a twinkle in her eye. "So, I'm just unlucky."

"It appears so, but ..." I paused. I wanted to keep her safe, but Rose was in such an optimistic place, I questioned whether or not to tell her she wasn't free from danger.

"But what?" Rose asked.

"When I interviewed John, I had the feeling he hadn't sent anyone after you. But my gut told me he wasn't done with you. I don't think he'll send someone, but I think once he's out of prison, he'll try to find you." I raised my hands. "To be fair, this is my gut, not hard evidence. But I would advise you to remain vigilant. Keep up with your training. Keep strong. And keep that great attitude."

With determination in her eyes, Rose said, "Oh, I will. If he comes for me, I'll be ready."

Rose was going to face her demon head-on. I needed to do the same. I tipped my chin, and a tiny grin made its way to my face. "I have no doubt."

We finished up the paperwork to close out the case, and she thanked me again as we hugged our good-byes.

CHAPTER TWENTY

MARTINA - THREE MONTHS LATER

Despite my aching muscles, I jogged toward the door where Rocco was waiting outside like a bouncer. My cross-fit class was clear across town and traffic had been a nightmare. I had contemplated skipping the class but knew that it was important to keep with my routine.

Since I started AA, Rocco had convinced me that to have a healthy mind, I also needed a healthy body. He explained that addicts tended to replace one harmful form of medication for another, like switching the booze for sugar and unhealthy comfort food. He insisted that although it'll make me feel good at the moment, it'd weigh me down, making me feel worse in the end. Not that I was ever really into junk food, but based on his advice, I'd adopted a new focus on my health, my body, and my mind.

I now attended the gym daily and ate a clean and healthy diet. No refined sugars. No trans fats. Zoey wasn't terribly pleased by the new regime, but she was adjusting, and I allowed for the occasional pizza and ice cream.

I felt stronger than I ever had before. In my younger army days, I was fit, but I don't remember ever feeling like this. I often thought of Rose even though I hadn't talked to her since our last meeting, but the transformation she had undergone in such a short amount of time really stuck with me. Now that it had been three months since my accident, like Rose, I didn't feel like my old self either. I felt better.

I reached Rocco, and he greeted me with a huge bear hug. I was no tiny lady at five feet eight inches tall, but he was massive. Although he didn't hang with Hells Angel's anymore, he still dressed mostly in jeans and black leather, looking like your typical scary dude. In reality, he was a big teddy bear. He placed me back down. "Are you ready for this?"

I grinned. "Absolutely." And I was. I worked hard to get here. Harder than I'd ever had to work in my entire life. My whole life, I'd felt strong and full of courage, but the last year made me see that we can't always be tough and hard. Sometimes things just rattle you to the core. They change who we are. God put me on this path, and I believe that I've endured the pain and the heartache for a higher purpose. Although sometimes it still feels quite senseless to have taken Jared, I feel like I'm becoming the woman I was intended to be.

Rocco pulled the door and held it open. "After you."

I entered the small assembly room of the local church. Chairs were lined up with the podium in the front. Snacks to the side. I didn't touch the donuts, but I did partake in the coffee. I was thankful it was one addiction I didn't have to break.

I marched to the front row of seats and sat myself down. Rocco sat next to me. I felt like I was bursting with energy. Heart racing, I prayed, *God, I hope I don't cry in front of everyone.*

After they called my name, I stepped up to the podium, head held high, and accepted my ninety-day chip. Before I began to speak about my journey and thank my fellow addicts, I spotted Stavros standing in the back corner of the room. Our eyes met, and he gave me an encouraging nod. I nodded back and took a moment to wipe the tears that escaped before I began to speak my gratitude.

It had been a rough few months. I'd started counseling, outpatient rehabilitation, and attended AA every day. I'd had to face the fact Jared was gone and not coming back. I'd had to learn how to manage my grief and desire for self-medication. I'd been forced to be vulnerable, something I didn't like to do, but I also understood that accepting help is a sign of strength. When the police came knocking to charge me with a DUI for the accident, I'd thought maybe my hard work had been in vain, but once again, Stavros had been right. The judge saw I'd been working the steps and decided to drop the charges.

When I wanted to give in, I pushed ahead, taking it one day at a time. I had to. For Zoey. For myself. For all the people who still needed my help. I still fought my demons each day, but like Rocco always reminded me, "We're all perfectly imperfect humans, and that's okay."

ALSO BY H.K. CHRISTIE

The Selena Bailey Series is a suspenseful series featuring a young Selena Bailey and her turbulent path to becoming a top notch kickass private investigator as led by her mentor, Martina Monroe.

Not Like Her, Book 1

One In Five, Book 2

On The Rise, Book 3

A Permanent Mark: A heartless killer. Weeks without answers. Can she move on when a murderer walks free? If you like suspenseful mysteries, you love this full length novel featuring a grown-up Selena Bailey.

Women's Fiction By Hannah K. Christie

The Unbreakable Series is a heart-warming women's fiction series, inspired by true events. If you like journeys of self-discovery, wounded heroines, and laugh-or-cry moments, you'll love the Unbreakable series.

We Can't Be Broken, Book 0

Where I'm Supposed To Be, Book 1

Change of Plans, Book 2

JOIN H.K. CHRISTIE'S READER'S CLUB

Join my reader club to be the first to hear about upcoming novels, new releases, giveaways, promotions, and more!

It's completely free to sign up and you'll never be spammed by me, you can opt out easily at any time.

To sign up go to
www.authorhkchristie.com

PLEASE LEAVE A REVIEW!

Thank you for reading *Crashing Down*! I hope you enjoyed reading it as much as I loved writing it. If you did, I would greatly appreciate if you could post a short review.

Reviews are crucial for any author and can make a huge difference in visibility of current and future works. Reviews allow us to continue doing what we love, *writing stories.* Not to mention, I would be forever grateful!

Thank you!

ABOUT THE AUTHOR

H. K. Christie watched horror films far too early in life. Inspired by the likes of Stephen King, Dean Koontz and a vivid imagination she now writes suspenseful thrillers featuring unbreakable women.

When not working on her latest novel, she can be found eating & drinking with friends, running slowly, or playing with her rescue pup, Mr. Buddy Founders.

She is a native and current resident of the San Francisco Bay Area.

ACKNOWLEDGMENTS

I'd like to thank my two ride or dies, aka, little sisters: Kaitlyn and Juliann for their early read and helpful feedback. My editor, Dawn, for keeping me on the right track. My cover artist, Suzana, for her wonderful designs. And as always a shout out to my husband, Jon, for enduring while I write while on every vacation and ignore my surroundings as I get words down on the page.